# CUT SHOT

John R. Corrigan

Sleeping Bear Press
310 North Main Street
P.O. Box 20
Chelsea, MI 48118
www.sleepingbearpress.com

Printed and bound in Canada.
10 9 8 7 6 5 4 3 2 1
Library of Congress Cataloging-in-Publication Data
Corrigan, J. R. (John R.)
Cut shot / by J.R. Corrigan.
p. cm.
ISBN 1-58536-028-7
1. Golfers—Fiction. 2. Gambling—Fiction I. Title.
PS3603.O685 C88 2001
813'.6—dc21
2001003935

# CUT SHOT

—

John R. Corrigan

Sleeping Bear Press

*For Lisa, Delaney, and Audrey*

*"It's a way to live. Anything else is confusion."*

ROBERT B. PARKER, *CEREMONY*


*"This above all: to thine own self be true;*
*And it must follow, as the night the day,*
*Thou canst not then be false to any man."*

WILLIAM SHAKESPEARE, *HAMLET*


*"Knights had no meaning in this game. It wasn't a game for knights."*

RAYMOND CHANDLER, *THE BIG SLEEP*

# Chapter One

——

I HAD HIT MY FINAL approach shot to within six feet of the pin and now stood on the 18th green, preparing to putt for a 68. March in Tucson typically means wind, and on this Thursday afternoon the flags were dancing. However, I was close to that sacred state where mind, body, and environment mesh. I had fired to within several feet of my intended targets all day and had rolled the ball equally well. At three under par, I was focused and confident— which made it even more difficult to watch Hutch Gainer.

Poor play can be contagious, so I had remained politely conversational, but kept my distance. He was a diminutive Texan who wore a Stetson hat and had a voice that twanged like piano wire. Usually he moved with a Lee Trevino swagger. Today, however, there was no spring in his step.

The green sloped front to back and Hutch's approach shot had left him below the cup. He leaned over a 10-footer—for an 80—and made an uncharacteristic stroke, a short jab. The ball ran eight feet past. The gallery reacted sympathetically.

My name is Jack Austin. I play the PGA Tour and suffer from a blessing called dyslexia. Growing up, no one knew much about it, and when it's sink or swim, you develop strategies. One of mine is to concentrate completely and channel every ounce of energy into one task at a time. On the golf course, where I make my living, I have mastered this. So I stood behind my ball marker, trying to get a read on my six-footer, while Hutch and our playing partner, Grant Ashley, decided who was away.

——

My line looked to be two feet right of the cup—a sidehill putt. I made several practice strokes, gently rocking my shoulders back and forth. The Arizona sun was warm on my back, the desert air was dry, and I was parched. My caddie, Tim Silver, had a master's in journalism and carried for me off and on, gathering information for a book about the Tour. He stood next to me holding the flagstick.

Hutch was still away, so he marked his ball and replaced it, aligning the logo so it would spiral if struck properly. He began to straighten, then fell to his knees, clutching his stomach.

I rushed over. "You O.K.?"

His Stetson hat lay before him on the green. His eyes were narrow and darted past me to the gallery.

"Hutch," I said, "what is it?" I was on all fours next to him.

"I need help," he said.

I yelled: "Get a doctor!"

"Not like that. *Your* help. It's eating me from the insides out."

"What is?"

We were surrounded quickly and Hutch climbed to his feet. "I'm O.K.," he said. "Just a cramp. I can putt out."

\* \* \*

At eight P.M., I sat across from Lisa Trembley, my fiancée, in the hotel restaurant. We were meeting for a late dinner.

"Sorry I'm late," I said.

"I just got here, too."

A waiter appeared and we ordered: fajitas for me; chicken salad, fat-free vinaigrette on the side for Lisa.

"Sixty-eight today, huh?" she said.

"Sixth place." In truth, it had been so long since I'd been in contention, seeing my name on the leader-board had left me nervous and exhilarated. "I putted well, been working on that."

"I know."

The scent of spice and flame was present and mixed with Lisa's soft perfume. The restaurant was typically Southwest: adobe walls; a low, round fireplace jetted from one corner; and the floor was red brick. The ceiling was lined with dark logs like an old western fort. Our seat cushions were made of woven straw.

Lisa was the lead golf analyst for CBS. On weekdays, she occasionally worked for USA Network and sat in the second chair next to Bill Macatee. At times she did on-course reporting and feature assignments. She was also the only one in the business to wear a suit every day. Now, however, she was in a white sleeveless silk top and blue jeans, in which she could pass for a college sophomore. Her features were tiny, the line of her jaw strong and well-defined, and her brown eyes were large and always seemed to hint of laughter to come.

I too had changed from work clothes—a golf shirt and khakis—into my relaxed attire: a fresh golf shirt and khakis.

"What happened on the 18th green?" she said.

"I don't know."

The waiter returned with our drinks. I was having a Heineken; Lisa had ordered a margarita.

"Hutch said he cramped up," she said tasting the margarita. She made a face.

"Strong?"

"Too strong. He denied my interview request. Probably still not feeling well."

At a table in the corner sat an elderly gray-haired man in a dark suit. Eating with him was a striking blond woman in a black cocktail dress, an olive-skinned man with a long ponytail, and Hutch Gainer. The old-timer made eye contact with me, nodded, and smiled.

"I wanted to ask Hutch about that two-footer he missed on 17," she said.

"I was shocked he missed it. It looked dead straight."

"And uphill. He just botched it. I thought he could talk about the distractions players face."

She picked up her glass by the stem, twirled it, and examined the salt on the edge. I was drinking from the bottle.

"I don't know," she said. "I talked to Hutch a couple hours after he was finished." She shook her head. "He looked awful, more upset than sick. He's just a kid. Maybe he's having a hard time."

I thought of Hutch's strange comment. He had finished with a three-putt 82. And yet he was one of the best putters I'd seen. The first day I had met him he took a hundred bucks from me playing "drawback" on the practice green. The kid was certainly distracted —no one with that stroke misses a kick-in two-footer unless something is weighing heavily on his mind; yet it wasn't his score that bothered me most. It was the fear I'd seen in his eyes before the crowd had gathered on the 18th green.

"Hutch looks fine now," she said, noticing him at the table in the corner.

\* \* \*

After dinner, our waiter appeared and asked if we'd like dessert. The menu ran to cheesecake. For a split second, I saw *hceesecake*. I refocused and saw *cheesecake*.

I chuckled.

"Sir, if there's something not on the menu, I can see if—"

"No, the menu looks fine," I said. "A slice of cheesecake to split."

"Low fat," Lisa said.

The waiter left.

"What was that about?" she asked.

"I almost asked the waiter what *hceesecake* was."

"What?"

"I reversed the first two letters of *cheesecake*."

She reached to pat my hand, but caught herself. "I almost did it again."

"Don't feel sorry for me," I said. "Dyslexia is a blessing."

"I know you feel that way."

The waiter came back with our *hceesecake*.

"Anything to drink with the cheesecake?" he said.

"Where I come from, we call it *heesecake*, with an H."

"Um," the waiter said, "heesecake it is, then, sir. Anything to go with the, ah, heesecake?"

"Ignore him," Lisa said. "Two glasses of skim milk, please."

When the waiter was gone, I shook my head. "You live on rabbit food. Be wild and crazy. Order a glass of whole milk."

"I was wild and crazy when I agreed to marry you." She picked up her fork and cut a wedge of cheesecake. "We've got to pick a date for the honeymoon. A lot depends on whether or not you qualify for the U.S. Open. NBC has that, so I have the week off anyway."

"If I win this week everything takes care of itself."

"So you're feeling good about your game?"

I paused while a waiter with a sizzling tray of fajitas passed.

"Extremely. I'm hitting the ball better than ever."

"And putting well," she said.

Her interest in my putting was legitimate: she had once done a segment on the breakdown of the putting stroke, featuring my motion as a model of what not to do.

"Everything's set for June 13th," she said. "The church, the priest, the dinner."

I took her hand. She was wearing the diamond I had bought.

She grinned and said: "I talked with your mother tonight. She said it was about time you got married, and when were we having kids."

It made me smile. The cheesecake was gone. I'd eaten two-thirds. "Want coffee?"

"You ready for bed?" she said.

"I'm not tired."

She looked around covertly, then back at me with a smirk. "Who said anything about sleep?"

* * *

After living hotel room to hotel room for years, I had finally been able to afford something more. I was in a suite and Lisa and I were on the balcony, side by side, forearms resting on the railing. Below us the back nine sprawled against the night sky. The moon was partially hidden behind one of the rugged mountain ranges that surrounded the city.

"What a view," she said.

"I've been on Tour for a decade and it's the first time I'm staying in a place like this."

"You work hard—lifting weights, hitting balls, putting—you earned that endorsement contract."

The moonlight reflected off the sand and lit the desert land-scape below. I thought of our lives, traveling city to city, living out of suitcases. Our romance had been something of a fairytale. I had always known professional sports prolonged adolescence; athletes don't live in the real world. The real world was that in which I had been raised: my father was a carpenter, my mother a substitute teacher. They had never earned more than $30,000 in a single year, yet had scraped to send their learning-disabled son to private school so he could have a college education.

As I thought of the suite and looked out at the velvet fairways below, I felt something very close to shame.

Lisa moved nearer to me and I rested my chin gently on her head, my arms around her waist. Her hair smelled of rain and lilac. I kissed her neck. She turned and draped both arms over my shoulders.

Moments later, beneath the covers, our hot breaths intermingled with short gasps and slow words. My hands caressed and moved over her body as if uncontrolled by impulses from my own brain. We made love. In my mind's eye, majestic, vivid colors appeared like a kaleidoscope: crisp hues of blue, cardinal and fire-truck reds, bright yellows, then pale and forest greens appeared and vanished behind my eyelids, rising and falling tenderly, like windswept flowers. Lisa's eyes were closed. Continually, her back and neck arched. Then her eyes opened and I felt her body tense and release.

Moments later I did the same.

Afterward, while she slept, I lay awake thinking of Hutch Gainer. So I began to reread Shakespeare's *King Lear*, the play about a man betrayed by his daughters, a betrayal he should've seen coming but did not grasp until it was too late. Shakespeare is not easy for anyone. For me, reading the 120-page play at my pace, that of a snail's, and reading while on Tour—sporadically—it takes no less than three weeks. But I read with a pen, concentrating, underlining, rereading passages because I want to understand the play. And I know each time I discover a little more. After a half-hour, I drifted to fitful sleep and dreamt of the play and Gloucester wandering through the woods blinded and helpless.

Then my eyes flickered and I woke. The alarm clock on the nightstand said 3:33. Someone was at the door. Lisa slept like the dead, so I got up without disturbing her and went to the front room, carefully closing the bedroom door behind me.

Hutch Gainer stood in the light of the hallway. Wearing only gray gym shorts, clutching a piece of white paper, he was barefoot, his hair disheveled, his boyish face looking weary. His puffy eyes darted from mine to the empty hallway over his shoulder. "I need help," he said for the second time.

# Chapter Two

——

I closed the balcony's sliding glass door behind us and stood, leaning on the railing.

I had expected Tim Silver and his fellow caddies, beer bottles in hand, wobbly after a long night at the bar, needing to discuss my putting problems or share golf tales. But the knock had not been theirs. Instead, it was Hutch. And he was not drunk. In fact he looked painfully sober, as he sat on a plastic deck chair.

"Can we go inside?" he said. "It's cold out here."

"Dress warmer. My fiancée is asleep in the bedroom. What is it?"

"Sweet Jesus," he said. "I thought CBS stayed across town. Lisa Trembley is in there?"

Many members of the press, including Lisa, had called him a can't-miss future star. He didn't look like one now. He had the color of a hung fish.

"What is it?" I said. "It's late."

He glanced at the sliding glass door like a condemned man eyeing the gallows.

"She's asleep," I said. "She can't hear us."

He exhaled slowly and looked out at the night. "I'm in trouble." His Texas drawl stretched syllables and made the words linger.

"What kind?"

Standing next to him, I could make out crossed golf clubs in the form of a dark tattoo on his left shoulder. His physique was that of a flyweight; likewise, his game was the antithesis of mine: he was ranked dead last in driving distance and first in putting.

He reached behind him, making sure the door was closed. "She's a shark, Austin."

When I had been a rookie, I had called people Sir.

"I got something to tell you that, like, she can't find out."

I spread my hands. "I'm engaged to be married to her, Hutch."

He ran a hand through his hair, looking at the paper.

"It's a quarter to four," I said. "You and I tee off early. Get on with it."

He exhaled and rolled his head side to side, cracking his neck. "No one can know."

On the golf course, this kid stood over five-footers to save par and yawned. In the locker room, he joked and told people, *Don't may-ass with Tayxas, man*. Now he looked ready for a coronary.

"Just tell me," I said.

He handed me the white sheet of paper.

"It's dark, Hutch. What's it say?"

"To shoot 75."

I held the note up, straining to read the typeface in the moonlight:

HUTCH,

SHOOT 75 OR HIGHER TOMORROW AND BOGEY THE 18TH. IF THOSE DEMANDS ARE NOT MET JOHN PICKORINO WILL FIND OUT WHAT YOU DID.

Hutch was nodding slowly.

"Who's Pickorino?" I said. "What did you do? Where'd you get this? And why aren't they asking for cash?"

"Under my hotel room door. It's always the same."

I crossed my arms. It was chilly standing against the evening breeze in only boxers. "Hutch, I'm no cop."

"I can't go to the cops. Pickorino owns cops."

"Who is he?" I said.

"Guy I was eating with. My sponsor."

"Your sponsor?"

"Yeah, but I can't keep doing it—my stomach is a mess—so I came to you. I didn't know where else to turn."

"I'm neither a doctor nor a cop," I said and shook my head. I had been awakened; it was not even four A.M.; it was dark; and I tried to comprehend it all. "How many times has this happened?"

"Like seven, eight."

"That explains the missed two-footer and the three-putt on 18."
He looked away.

"Always to throw strokes, never for cash?"

"I'd rather pay."

"Anyone would. So nearly 10 times you've cheated?"

"I said seven, maybe eight—and it's just to drop shots. Not like cheating to win." He leaned back in his chair and absently rubbed his lower stomach. "Maybe the players wouldn't care. They're making more money because of it."

"People don't work their whole lives to play the Tour so you can give them strokes, Hutch. Plenty of guys would want to kick your ass. They'd probably appreciate it if I did it myself."

"Pickorino will kill me, Jack. People talk about how you were a crime writer."

"I covered a police beat for a newspaper once, Hutch. I was an English major in college, but that doesn't mean I'm going to lecture at Harvard."

"I didn't know who else to go to."

"What exactly is going on? Somebody's betting if they're asking you to throw strokes."

"I don't know."

"What's Pickorino got on you?"

"Will you help me?"

"Answer the question."

He exhaled slowly. The chair scraped on the cement. He was fidgeting. "Golf is all I know, you know? I was 17, moved from Houston to New Orleans. Buddy of mine was working at a club and, like, he said they needed an assistant pro. Never wanted to be a club pro, but I was a scratch player. Figured it'd give me a chance to practice a lot. Maybe hustle."

With those aspirations, I thought, it was no wonder we were having this conversation.

"So, I go out there and one day I give a lesson to this old-timer. And it's strange. He wears a suit jacket to the lesson and, like, gives it to this big spic to hold while he's hitting."

"I find that term offensive," I said.

"Sorry. Anyway, he pays me the 30 bucks for the half-hour, then tips me 20. I don't have any money, so a 20-buck tip? I'm thinking, like, this guy's the balls, you know?"

"The balls," I said.

"I give him some more lessons. Then one day he says he can't play on the course, but he's hitting it pretty good during lessons. I tell him I can give a playing lesson—mostly because playing 18 is better than renting carts all afternoon."

The darkness was fading. "We tee off in five hours, Hutch."

"So, we play. I give him some pointers—a preswing routine, reading the greens, club selection, that stuff. Well, one day he comes in the pro shop. Says he's got a match and he'll pay me four hours of lessons if I caddie for him and help him out. Now I don't even know who this guy is."

"Who is he?"

"John Pickorino. Head of a Mafia family in Orleans. I don't know anything about that stuff. I go out and he wins his bet and tips me an extra hundred. A hundred-buck tip, Jack. I didn't think much about it then, but obviously he tips me a hundred, he's, like, playing for a lot of dough. Anyway, he wins so he wants me to caddie for him all the time."

"And you enjoy the money."

"Of course, so I do it and he starts, like, taking me to dinner, watching me play in local tournaments."

"And you still don't know this guy's occupation?"

"No. I figured it out, but he says he'll put up four grand for Qualifying School, and if I get a Tour card, says he'll sponsor me till I get my feet on the ground."

Things were getting clearer. "You did something that somebody could hold over you. What was it?"

Beneath his lip, Hutch ran his tongue along his upper teeth. He looked down at the floor, then back at me. "I still don't know, like, who's playing in these matches, you understand?" he said.

"You should know how to take care of yourself."

"Hey, listen, Austin, I didn't come here for a lecture."

"Then leave." I pointed to the door. "I don't know what you expected coming here in the first place."

He ignored that. "A guy comes in, gives me two grand to help him out—give Pickorino the wrong club, a bad read on the green here and there. I needed the money."

"Needed or enjoyed?"

"Huh?"

"So you sell out the old man?" I said.

"These guys are, like, throwing a lot of dough at me. I got no family, no silver spoon. I'm on my own." In the moonlight, I could see a line of sweat appearing on his forehead.

"Touching," I said.

"Hey—"

"No," I said. "Let me get this straight: you come out here on Pickorino's coin, start to win, and someone begins blackmailing you?"

"Yeah."

"How much did Pickorino lose?"

His head shook back and forth slowly. "He was playing for big money, Jack."

"How much?"

"Couple million."

"You cheated him out of two million bucks, then you take his money as your sponsor? You *ought* to be scared. Who paid you off?"

"That's the thing. A different guy every time."

"Same family?"

The sky was turning gray now as he shook his head. I saw his eyes get large and blank, as if he had momentarily left the balcony and traveled back to when he had made these decisions.

"You're certain it wasn't the same family?" I asked.

"Pickorino would talk about it. 'I beat so-and-so last week,' and he'd call them some nickname—the squid heads, if they worked out of a seafood place. He'd call another guy something else. That was what made it a big deal. It was like a tour to him. He beat the other families."

"How many were there?"

"I said, like, I don't know about that stuff."

"Think."

"A total of seven or eight times. Always a different guy would pay me."

"And Pickorino never played against the same family. The proverbial needle in the haystack."

Hutch stood and leaned on the rail beside me.

It was too early for this. *King Lear* provided all the mental stimulation I had needed for one evening. But Hutch was just a kid, an early season favorite for Rookie of the Year. How had he gotten into this? And so masterful in the mystical art that was putting; Hutch Gainer was the best I'd ever seen.

And now I had lost all respect for the guy.

He turned around and shuffled back to his chair, sat, and ran a hand through his hair. His chin dropped to his pale chest. Tears ran down his cheeks.

"I can't do it any more," he said. "It's not golf, you know?"

"Throwing strokes?" I crossed my arms and spat over the railing. "Naw, Hutch. It would make a good slogan for the Tour: *play golf like the pros, let your buddies win.* Or they could change the one we have—*These guys are good*—to *These guys are greedy*."

"Hey, man—"

"Shut up," I said. "I'm trying to make a living here and you show up at this hour the night before the second round? This isn't something I can fix. You're worried Pickorino will show up at your room and—"

"He travels with me. We share a room."

I began to speak, then stopped. "You room with him?"

"That's why I came this late. He's asleep. His girlfriend's here and I'm staying next door with his limo driver, the spic."

"I asked you not to use that term."

"Sorry. Hispanic."

"You don't dare just pay him what you owe for expenses and send him home?"

"I heard people call him 'Johnny Pick' because he ice-picked some guy who owed him money. And he loves being out on Tour—thinks he's, like, a player or something, walking around, talking to people. I'm not doing anything to stir the pot."

"Pickorino doesn't know about the notes?"

"They shove them under my door. Sometimes I'm asleep. But he's never there when they come."

"Convenient."

The sun was an orange splash on the backs of the distant mountains now. We were talking about the Mafia; pride was more important than money. And Hutch had used this man badly.

"Listen," I said, "forget the notes and try to win enough money to pay him back."

"No way," he said. "That's suicide."

"Pickorino might never find out."

He was standing next to me again. "'Might' isn't good enough, Austin."

My last name again. I took a deep breath and thought about it all: what he had done, and what it could mean to the Tour's reputation. I felt my face redden.

"Can you help me or not?"

"I gave you advice."

"That's not advice. Austin, man, help me."

I hit him with an uppercut to the stomach and felt his body contract and rise. Then he dropped, landing on all fours on the cement.

He gasped: "The hell...was that...for?"

"For the guys who stay on the range until their hands bleed," I said. "For them."

"I needed money."

"We all did. You've brought the goddamned Mafia and illegal gambling to the Tour."

"Fine." He got to his feet like an old man. "This is life or death. But I'll handle it."

When he fumbled with the sliding glass door, I had to let him out.

# Chapter Three

—

I HADN'T BEEN ABLE TO FALL back to sleep after he had left. I lay in bed thinking of him, of gambling, and of the Tour. It had all brought back what had been a rite of passage for me, a time, many years earlier, when my father and I had driven his rusted pickup down a dirt road to a nine-hole municipal course in western Maine. My father, who played maybe once a week, had taken the game up later in life but had fallen in love with it. He was a stocky man who wore flannel shirts and had the thick callused hands of a laborer. Yet he possessed the necessary depth to have seen the allegory the game offered and the perception to have discovered what lay beneath its surface.

It was late afternoon, the air was humid, and we sat on a bench waiting for the group in front of us to clear the fairway. I was nine years old and my father's large arm, which was now wrapped around me, meant more than anything. The conversation was one I would never forget:

He leaned back, his long legs in tan work pants stretched out before him. "What did you get on that hole, Jack?"

"A five," I said, my feet dangling an inch or so off the ground.

"You had a five, huh?"

"Yup."

"That's a really good score, son. I made seven. Do you like golf?"

"Oh, yes."

"That's great," he said. "You know golf is a man's game, Jack. Do you know what I mean by that?"

—

"Uh huh."

"I mean in how a man acts—self-respect, dignity, honesty. A golfer has those things. When I go into someone's house to build cabinets or put up a wall, no one has to tell me to do a good job or to be honest. I do the best I can because it's the right thing to do. Did you do the best you could on that hole?"

"Yes."

"And was that a five?"

It had taken me a long time to answer. My father worked very hard; even at that young age I had known that. Slowly, I shook my head. "Ten."

I felt his hand rub the back of my head and we talked some more. But those lines were the ones I had never forgotten. As I lay staring at the ceiling, listening to Lisa's breath and thinking of Hutch Gainer and John Pickorino and wondering what fans of the game and the legends who had forged the life I now was living would think if they knew Hutch's poor play was not accidental— those lines replayed over and over in my head. Hutch Gainer was doing everything wrong. And he was too scared to stop.

And he had come to me for help.

*  *  *

At daybreak, I was on the driving range, completely alone. I was swinging too hard; my body couldn't catch up with my hands. Cursing Hutch Gainer, I sent a drive out beyond the 300-yard marker and held my follow-through to watch the ball's trajectory against the rising sun.

I was running on three hours of sleep, but my mind still raced. I had met Hutch playing drawback—a practice-green game in which every putt missed is pulled back the length of your putter. It is designed to strengthen your stroke but I had turned it into a money match because I seem to always seek additional competition. So I had gambled on golf myself. And no different from my draw-back match with Hutch, I routinely played practice rounds on Tuesdays for money against fellow Tour players. Was I better than the people blackmailing Hutch?

I hit three more shots and mulled over that question.

Yes, I was. Money matches had long been a part of golf, a way for competitive people to add an additional stake. It had, to a degree, taught me to play under pressure. Lee Trevino once said that pressure is playing for $10 when you've only got $5 in your pocket. What I was speaking of was creating competition; what Hutch was doing, and what he was too frightened to stop doing, was cheating. The blackmailers were using him to lessen the sport, not raising the competitive bar. Indeed, no one threw strokes when you had to pull out your own wallet, look the guy in the eye, and hand him your money. No. One was competition; the other was cheating for someone else's profit—the question was whose.

It was now close to seven and time to put Hutch out of my mind. With a ball positioned off my left instep, I took the club away slowly, my weight shifting to my right, my back leg stiffening; I paused with the club overhead, nearly parallel to the ground, then my weight shifted forward, my back leg flexed and pushed down and left; the club descended, my right elbow brushing my side, powering through as my wrists rotated and snapped the ball airborne.

I caught it flush.

The three-iron carried over 220 yards before floating down and bounding out of sight in a spray of morning dew. We called that "pure-ing" it, the contact so rare that sometimes the sensation sent chills up and down my arms; today, it merely helped clear my head.

* * *

Brian "Padre" Tarbuck had jade-blue eyes and the stubble of a beard that—on my face—would look like a five-day growth. On him, women found it sexy. On occasion, female fans followed him back to his hotel. And, on occasion, they left the following morning—a tremendous contrast to his nickname, which spawned from his former profession: he had been a priest.

"Swinging for the fences?" He sipped coffee from a paper cup.

"I'm smoothing it out," I said and leaned on my club.

"You better slow that down. We've got to turn things around."

"We? You won last year. I don't have a two-year exemption."

"I still owe it to God to do the best I can. I haven't played up to my potential lately."

I put my golf bag on its side and sat on the end.

"Speaking of doing your best," he said, "you play in the Hutch Gainer group yesterday?"

"I like to think of it as the Jack Austin group."

"What's going on with that kid? He won twice his first month on Tour."

"And?"

"And he blew three shots on the 18th green yesterday."

"Must be a slump," I said. Could people tell Hutch had thrown strokes? What was the word in the locker room?

"He's playing bad. Ought to talk to somebody, get a lesson."

"Tell him that," I said.

"I will."

I wanted to know where this was coming from. "You giving anybody who plays a bad round a lecture?"

"The kid has too much talent to waste it." He sipped more coffee. "That three-putt on 18 was horrendous."

"Told me he's got a kink in his stroke."

"Something's off," he said. "Want to have a drink tonight?"

"I'll see if Lisa has anything planned." When I three-putted a green, people yawned. This conversation told me one thing: people knew Hutch shouldn't be three-putting. And that made me nervous.

Padre was smiling. "Jack, you know I, of all people, understand the weighty seriousness and fully respect the vows of marriage—"

"Yeah?"

The smile became a wide-eyed smirk. "—but you're whipped."

"And you're jealous."

"Lisa Trembley?" he said. "Of course, I am." He walked off.

* * *

Tim Silver arrived next, wearing his white poncho that had AUSTIN in bold black lettering on the back. His goatee was neatly trimmed and his shaved head shone.

"Your shirt's soaked. What time you get here?"

My white golf shirt had TITLEIST on the right breast and left sleeve. The collar hung low with perspiration.

He handed me a towel and I wiped my face. He turned the bag upright. My name was on the front, TITLEIST was on one side, and *Golf Weekly* was on the other. Silver rummaged through the pockets and retrieved a small notebook.

"Couldn't sleep," I said.

"You need practice anyway."

"It's nice when your caddie's encouraging."

He flipped through pages and glanced up. "I call it like I see it, Whitebread."

"I had a 68 yesterday."

"I can say what I want. I'm a bargain."

He was. Most nonsalaried caddies get roughly $900 a week,

then five to ten percent of winnings. Silver was getting a flat $300 and total access to players and life on Tour for his book.

Behind him, standing on the other side of a rope separating the range from the gallery, I recognized John Pickorino, Hutch's dinner partner, sponsor, and the man he had helped lose two million bucks. He wore a tan suit. Next to him was the Latino man with a long black ponytail I'd seen at dinner. The limo driver. He looked to be late 20s and wore a black satin windbreaker, black jeans, and black snakeskin boots. He stood, arms crossed, staring at me.

"You hit it a long way," Pickorino said, smiling.

I shrugged modestly.

"But don't watch him putt," Silver said and smirked.

"Cute," I said.

Pickorino chuckled and both men went and watched two other players. I followed them with my eyes and considered the odd visit.

Silver apparently hadn't thought anything seemed strange.

"You know what those suits run?" he said.

"You're the fashion police. Tell me."

"Around fifteen-hundred."

"A little warm for the golf course."

"Got to make sacrifices if you want to look good, Jack."

"Guy with Mr. Suit is wearing black satin," I said. "Ugly and hot."

"True. But I've always liked tall, dark, and handsome. Like Eric Estrada."

"Do we have to constantly discuss your love fantasies?"

"Have I mentioned Montel Williams? You seen those buns?"

"I've got to get back to work."

\* \* \*

At eight A.M., the desert sun was already petulant. I had moved to the practice green, which was now full of players and surrounded by fans. Lisa, wearing a porcelain blue jacket over a white top and cropped pants that matched the jacket, was standing next to Ernie Els. She held a microphone as he spoke. Across from them, a cameraman stood, recording the interview. It had been how I had met her; suit and all, she frequently left the tower before the telecast to interview players herself. The additional information, she told me, allowed her to add flavor to her commentary when she resumed her spot in the tower.

I positioned three balls four feet from a cup. I made two of three, then stretched my back.

"How are you putting this week?"

Straightening, I saw Pickorino standing maybe 10 yards away, outside the rope which blocked off the putting green. I played along. "Putting's not too bad," I said. Naturally, I missed my next attempt.

He didn't comment.

I walked over and extended my hand. "Jack Austin."

His vice-like grip was dry and belied his age. "John Pickorino. I know who you are." He sounded like Sean Connery and spoke slowly and pronounced each syllable with care, a National Public Radio voice.

"Not many people do."

"Modesty is a good quality. You are one of the Tour's longest hitters. You rank fifth in driving distance."

"You must follow the Tour closely." Behind him people moved in and out, jockeying for position. Tiger had emerged from the locker room, putter in hand, and was walking toward the green.

"But you are nearly last in putting," Pickorino said, "as you just demonstrated." His lined face broke into a smile.

He watched Tiger and said: "You think anyone can beat the mooley?"

"Excuse me?"

"Tiger. Think anyone can beat him?"

"I know one player for sure," I said.

He leaned a little closer. He had a two-inch scar under one eye.

I smiled modestly and he realized whom I had meant. I saw the disappointment in his face. "And don't call him that," I said.

He straightened and frowned. In the pocket, where a display hankie should have been, was a small notepad.

"What's that?" I said.

"Oh, nothing." He put the pad in the inside breast pocket.

"We were in Vegas last week," I said. "Put any money on me?"

"You mean gamble?"

"Sure." We were sparing now.

He looked to the Latino. "No. Kiko and I are just fans. How did you fare?"

Across the green, I saw Lisa walking toward me, smirking broadly. As she approached several players grinned as well. We all knew what was coming.

"Missed the cut," I said to Pickorino. "But don't bet against me this week."

Kiko shifted. "Like Mr. Pickorino said, Bub, we don't gamble."

"Bub?"

"You heard me."

"Kiko, that's enough," Pickorino said. "Gambling is illegal in this state, Mr. Austin."

"Figure of speech," I said.

"Certainly. Play well today." He turned and walked away. Kiko stood staring at me momentarily, then followed.

Lisa was waiting for me next to Silver near the hole where I had been practicing. In deep thought, I returned to my practice station. Pickorino was feeling me out. And how could he not be present each time Hutch had received threats?

"Who was that?" Lisa said.

"Fans," I said.

She looked at Silver and grinned, a large eager grin, as if she genuinely wanted to help me. I knew she did not. And, when she felt enough players had gathered, she took the putter from my hand before I could object.

Around us, players leaned on their clubs. Some smiled. Some played along, stoically.

"Honey," she said, "you're taking the putter back too far inside."

The chuckling began.

"This," she demonstrated, making a jerky outside-to-in stroke, pushing it off line, "is your stroke."

I laughed. "I think I've got it under control."

"Let me show you—"

She took the second ball and drained a six-footer.

The muffled laughter was now full out.

"It's an easy game, Sweetie. I'll take a break later and help you some more."

"This is all the help I can handle in one morning."

She looked once more at her audience, grinned with the enthusiasm of a performer taking a bow, then walked toward the TV tower above the 18th hole. When she was out of earshot, it began:

"Honey," someone said, "you're taking the putter back too far inside."

"And take out the garbage."

"Then mow the lawn."

"And cook dinner."

The green erupted with laughter.

"She's a pistol," I said.

# Chapter Four

———

On the first tee, the air was warm and dry as dust. Anxiety always seems to make it difficult to breathe before my first shot. And the heat only added to that. I went through my breathing routine several times — in deeply through the nose, out the mouth. I was 35 and the game had always been, as Chi Chi Rodriguez says, more fun for me than any thing else you do with clothes on; yet even after a decade on Tour, the first shot of a competitive round still made me nervous.

Our threesome was the same as the day before — Hutch, Grant Ashley, and myself — and each of us was preparing. Grant and his caddie, Stump Jones, stood reviewing a yardage book; Hutch was next to caddie Fur Lomax, staring at the ground. Under the Arizona sun, in his hat, Hutch looked like Garth Brooks, except smaller and much more tired.

I exhaled deeply one last time and Silver and I walked to the others. We shook hands and were introduced via a PA system: "Now on the first tee, Jack Austin."

"Show time," Silver said, as he had on the first hole every time he caddied for me.

I pulled the three-wood from my bag, took two practice swings, then addressed the ball. The first hole was a 440-yard dogleg left. The fairway was lined with spectators and turned left at 275 yards; from there, it was 165 to the center of a pear-shaped green. On this day, the pin was tucked in the back left, behind a bunker.

I made a good pass at my Titleist and sent it about 280 yards

———

down the left side of the fairway, through the dogleg, just short of the right rough, leaving a short iron to the green. Being long off the tee has its advantages: it can set up a hole very nicely.

\* \* \*

Walking down the first fairway, Hutch moved beside me. Silver was chatting with Grant about going from college golf to the Tour and had moved out of earshot.

"Sorry about last night," Hutch said. "I shouldn't have, like, dragged you in."

"Don't dump strokes today."

"Jack," his voice was a whisper, "I have to."

"Don't do it."

He stopped and looked hard at me. "You'll help?"

I stopped as well, and scanned the gallery. My father's words played again. "Yes."

"How?"

"I don't know."

"But—"

"That's it," I said. "Shoot your best score." I moved away.

\* \* \*

The Gila Rancho Resort had recently been built and its course was a "stadium golf course," designed specifically for Tour events, which meant spectators lined each fairway on steep grass embankments. Waiting for Grant to hit to the first green, I saw Pickorino, Kiko, and the blond woman from dinner. She must've been Pickorino's girlfriend but looked more like his daughter.

When we arrived at my ball, I pulled an eight-iron, bent, and tossed some grass into the air. No breeze. I wanted to swing hard, about 95%. On this day, I had to establish an aggressive mind-set immediately. For a month, I had been playing conservatively—and not playing well. And this swing was aggressive.

The ball flew high and straight. I couldn't see it land because of an undulation in the green, but the gallery's reaction told me it was close.

On the green, I marked my 10-footer and watched as Hutch played a shot from the right rough. It looked easy enough—a pitch-and-run with a lot of green to work with. Choke down on an eight- or nine-iron and hit down on the ball; it should pop out and run toward the flag. I saw Hutch glance uneasily at Pickorino as he made several practice strokes. Then he chili-dipped it.

The ball jumped up, landed, and stopped six inches from where it had begun. As he tossed his club back into his bag and got another, he wouldn't look at me.

"Focus, Hutch. Concentrate," Pickorino said.

Hutch eyed the gallery and Pickorino gave a fatherly thumbs-up.

On the second try, he put the ball within three feet, then tapped in for bogey. He glanced at me. I spat and went to my ball.

I hadn't earned a cent in a month—four consecutive missed cuts. This was the first hole of the second round, and I was on the green in regulation, putting for a birdie. I had an opportunity to get off to a fast start.

My new Bullseye putter had been acquired at a yard sale in Orlando. Titleist owns Bullseye and Titleist craftsman Scotty Cameron had seen me using it and offered a newer model. I had declined; it was old, the face pockmarked with battle scars, but very heavy so it held the line back and through.

"Looks straight." Silver was crouched behind the ball. I was off to the side, looking at the slope of the green.

"But I'd still play it a couple inches to the left," he said.

"Not bad for an amateur."

He walked over and whispered: "You meant to say *cute* amateur."

"I've got to get a straight caddie," I said.

I went through my prestroke routine: crouched behind the ball, selected a line over which to roll it, stood, took two practice strokes while looking at the hole to get a feel for distance, thus the speed; then I addressed the ball and stroked it. It took the slight break Silver had noticed and dived into the cup.

I played the front nine well and went out in 34.

* * *

Walking up the 18th fairway, I moved to Hutch, who was alone and walking slowly. I pointed to a volunteer carrying our scores on a small sign. Hutch was four over par.

"That last shot looked like a 36 handicapper hit it," I said. He was lying three and a two-putt would give him his bogey on 18. "Make this putt, Hutch."

He squinted. We stopped and stood like that. His chin to his chest, he shook his head back and forth once, then walked away.

I walked to the 18th green, where Pickorino stood in the

gallery behind the hole. His hands were clasped behind him and he nodded at me. I didn't return the gesture. My name was on the leader-board and I was putting for birdie. Hutch knew what I thought. Now I had to worry about my own score and my putt, an uphill 12-footer.

My approach shot had been where I wanted it, below the hole. It's all part of course management—something I had grasped with the ease of a Doberman learning to be a vegetarian. When younger, I tried to drive every green. On occasion, I reached some of them. But watching guys like Tom Kite and Curtis Strange, you quickly notice they can't hit the ball as far as Tiger Woods or John Daly, but they can and do score like them. It's course management, thinking man's golf.

I stood over my putt and carefully aligned my shoulders to the hole. I set the putter behind the ball, took a deep breath, and stroked. This putt caught the right edge, did a complete 360, and rolled back two feet toward me. I tapped in and matched my front-nine score, shooting 68 for the second consecutive day. It was good for a share of fourth place. I knew it would be tough for those with afternoon tee times to catch me: the sun would bake the greens firm and four hours of spike marks would only add to the difficulty.

I had made my first cut in what seemed an eternity.

Hutch was next to putt. I watched as he did what he normally did—nothing. It was all natural to him. He simply stood over the ball—his Zebra putter resting gently in his hands, the line and speed obvious to him—and stroked.

The ball stopped six feet short of the hole. The gallery moaned with sympathy.

"Tough green," Grant said.

Again, I spat.

"Don't rush," Pickorino said.

Except Hutch always looked effortless on the green and Pickorino had seen him play more than I. Wouldn't he know Hutch didn't take a lot of time on the green?

Again I thought of how Pickorino, supposedly, had no knowledge of the blackmail notes. According to Hutch, he'd been a New Orleans organized crime figure for a long time. Guys don't last long in that business without keen observation skills.

Hutch leaned over his six-footer. When he brought the putter back, his hands twitched and he knocked it two feet past the hole. He tapped in for a double-bogey six—one better than the letter had demanded.

After Grant Ashley had putted out, I shook his hand, and turned to shake with Hutch. His face was ghostly white, and there were tears in his eyes. Suddenly his cheeks expanded, his hand shot up to cover his mouth, and he raced toward the locker room.

I followed.

* * *

With Hutch in a stall vomiting loudly, there was nothing for me to do. So I sat before my locker, a damp towel draped around my neck, my golf shirt soaked with perspiration, and watched the afternoon TV coverage. My 68 made Lisa's "earlier highlights" segment.

Several golfers were in the locker room, finished with their rounds, either preparing to shower, or heading to the range for practice. Each paused and looked toward the bathroom when they heard Hutch.

Phil Smits was five-foot-ten by five-foot-ten, balding, with pale blue eyes. We shook hands. The player with him, I didn't know.

"Who's in there?" Smits said.

"Hutch Gainer," I said. "Had a bad burger last night."

"Sounds like it."

"This is Mike Mikhailov."

I shook his hand.

"Call me Mickey," he said. "I went through Q School with Hutch. He all right?"

"Yeah," I said. "He'll be fine."

"I'm giving Mickey a lesson," Smits said.

"I lost a couple drives to the right—practically slicing it."

"On Tour," I smiled, "we call it an overcalculated fade."

He grinned. "And every time you miss a putt—"

"Tap the green with your putter," I said, "like the ball hit somebody's spike mark."

"Don't tell the rookies that, Jack," Smits said. "They're the ones we blame the spike marks on."

We all laughed.

I sat back down and watched them go. It was something that I believed separated golf from other sports: not only the veteran-rookie camaraderie, but two competitors helping each other. On Tour, if an area of your game is hurting, you can count on almost anyone you ask to give a lesson. When one considers that the ensuing lesson might take money from the pocket of the player giving it, it's easy to see why golf is a gentleman's game. In a sport that demands the every-man-for-himself attitude, the camaraderie is not only unique but also tremendous. It stems from a Tour-wide mutual respect. Players appreciate the fact that everyone is here to compete against the best of the best, to see how they stack up, to take their best shot. Which reminded me again of Hutch and made my stomach turn.

* * *

Hutch walked out of the bathroom as I was finishing my second bottle of water and watching Lisa on TV. I loved to watch her on TV. She was confident and beautiful. She was both of those off-screen, too, but when I saw her on TV, I knew men across the country were envious, which was a nice ego boost. There was something about her—holding her hand, or even simply watching her on TV—that gave me the sensation I'd had as a kid when I'd returned from college. In a profession where one travels city-to-city, 10 months per year, Lisa Trembley was the closest thing I had to a home.

Hutch stood before me and wiped his face on a towel. He was gray and blotchy.

"There's drool on your chin," I said.

He wiped it. "You waiting for me?"

"Yeah," I said.

He lowered his voice. "What do you want?"

"What do I want? I wouldn't mind kicking your ass, Hutch."

He said something I tuned out. The locker room still had players going to and fro. I wouldn't discuss this publicly.

One guy called over to Hutch and asked how he was.

"Food poisoning," I said. "Picked up a bad burger last night."

Hutch quickly nodded.

"Follow me," I said.

We went past the showers into a maintenance closet.

"What are we doing?" he said. "I'm like tired and sick."

"Stop whining and saying 'like.'"

There was a single white light bulb hanging from the ceiling. The walls were lined with metal shelving, and the floor was cement. The room seemed cold compared to the locker room. The air felt nice.

"Look, Jack, I don't have time. Pickorino will be looking—"

"You don't know a thing about this game or this Tour. I don't know if that's because you're young or just really stupid and selfish."

"Hey—"

I pushed his chest weakly, but it got his attention.

"Listen, Hutch, you came to me for help. I don't like what you did to the old man, Mafia or not. And I don't like you cheating us. But I don't want the game dragged through the mud."

"What mud?"

"Press. There's a gambling ring somewhere revolving around the Tour."

"Pickorino?"

"Probably. You said Pickorino's Mafia, and no one's asking you for cash. That's gambling and Mafia means big-money gambling."

"You going to ask Lisa to keep it out of the press?"

"She can't and wouldn't. And I wouldn't ask her to."

Outside the closet, I heard a shower start.

"This is how it'll work," I said. "I've got a friend who might help. He's a private investigator and you'll pay his fee."

I knew Perkins would never turn down my request for help. We were best friends. But I felt bad asking him to get mixed up in this. If I'd learned anything on the police beat it was that the mob doesn't appreciate invasions of privacy. Plus, Perkins and wife Linda had just had their first child—my Godson, Jackie. I didn't like the thought that this could get dangerous.

"I'm not doing this for you," I said. "Let's get that straight right now. Some guys who respect the game and appreciate the Tour—Nicklaus, Palmer, Player, Trevino—worked damned hard to put golf where it is, so guys like me can make a good living playing."

He was looking at the door.

"You know what the purse was at the very first tournament, Hutch? Seventy-five bucks. Total. A lot of guys worked too hard building this to have a young snot-nosed hustler disgrace the game."

"I didn't disgrace—"

I hit him in the chest again. This time he took three steps back.

"You got yourself into this mess. I'm just going to try to stop the blackmail, so it doesn't get to the press." As soon as I had said it, I thought of my fiancée and how she would be my largest obstacle.

"I told you, Pickorino will kill me."

"You deal with him yourself," I said and walked out.

# Chapter Five

——

IT WAS COOL AND COMFORTABLE when I went jogging Friday at eight P.M. Wearing gray New England Patriots shorts, a white T-shirt that said Titleist, and Adidas Falcon sneakers, I ran an east-south-west-north circle around the Gila Resort community where we were staying outside of Tucson. The resort was self-sufficient; it included a bustling main street and a "downtown" area.

The sun had set and the sky was clear and royal blue. A half-moon was already visible, and the air was dry. I realized I hadn't sweat much or, if I had, it had dried too quickly for me to notice. I was to meet Lisa for a late dinner. She had wanted to run with me, but had several interviews scheduled.

As fate would have it, I would be glad she had not come.

Running was not something that came easily. At six-foot-one, my weight fluctuated from 215 to 225. I didn't possess the physique of a sleek Kenyan marathoner; my build was more suited to weight lifting, which, in fact, I enjoyed. So, I had to run three days a week to stay in shape. If not, running became as enjoyable as a root canal.

On my final lap, I noticed a dark sedan heading slowly toward me as I went west.

It pulled to the curb opposite me.

Two men—wearing half-zipped jackets over T-shirts, jeans, baseball hats, and sunglasses—climbed out of the rear doors and headed in opposite directions on the sidewalk. They stopped about a hundred yards apart, one at each end of the block.

The car jumped back into traffic, U-turned, and stopped

behind me. Over my shoulder, in the reflection of a store window, I saw another guy, dressed similarly, get out and stand at that end of the block. Finally, the dark sedan rolled past me, pulled to the curb on my side of the street, and dropped the last man. All four quadrants were covered. I was the lone person between the two on my side of the street. Less than 50 yards separated me from either of them.

Tucson is not LA, New York, or Chicago. But anyone who plays golf for a living trusts his instincts. I stopped in front of a coffee shop, grabbed one ankle and stretched my quadriceps; it gave me a chance to think. The pit of my stomach held the strained sensation of being in the wrong place at the wrong time.

I looked down the block at the guy facing me. He stood, looking in my direction, one hand inside his jacket. That was all I needed. Something was going on and I wasn't sticking around to see what it was, or for whom it was meant. I would go inside, call the cops about suspicious activity, and drink a bottled water.

I started toward the coffee shop, and glanced at the guy in front of me. He was in a full sprint. The two across the street were converging. I heard footsteps coming from behind.

From that point, as if trying to recall a dream sequence, the memories become blurred:

Through the open door, into the crowded coffee shop. People staring, pointing. I hear nothing. Then my own voice: "Call the cops."

A pimple-faced kid across the counter doesn't answer.

I scream: "There a back exit?"

"For staff—"

I'm over the counter, sprinting toward the back.

"Hey. You can't—"

I'm running, crashing into containers, employees, and shelving. Behind me, someone yells, *"He's got a gun."* The back door is like a finish line and I burst through it, into a well-lit alley. Instantly, I realize it's like a tunnel, a shooter's haven—the sides lined with overflowing dumpsters. *Leap into one? No. Burrowing out of sight will take too long.*

Still sprinting, I bolt toward Main Street. My sweat-drenched clothing is heavy now; my feet like dumbbells. I hear my breath rasp in and out, my movements like slow motion. The alley's entrance is getting closer. My mind races. *If I can get to the street, I can make it.*

Then two men, the ones from the other side of the street, step in front of me, guns leveled.

One guy goes to his knee—a shooter's stance. The other drops his back foot, squares his shoulders, and aligns me with the sight at the end of his pistol.

I froze.

"Don't move, Austin," the guy standing said. His dark hair was worn long; a two-day growth covered his face.

Instinctively, my tongue ran along my upper lip. I tasted salt. Behind me, I heard the door open and footsteps. Two others in hats, glasses, and jackets. I'd never pick them out of a lineup.

Beard said: "Date a foxy reporter, huh?"

I said nothing.

"Know why I don't like media types?" he said.

"The big words they use?"

Shooting Stance grinned. "I think he's making fun of you."

I glanced over my shoulder. The other two were closer, so there was no way I could get to the street or back into the coffee shop.

Beard put his gun inside his coat, then reached behind him and retrieved a six-inch metal pipe. "I don't like media types cause they can't mind their own business."

I heard shuffling and glanced behind me. They were within punching distance now. I turned sideways so I was square to no one but could see all four.

Beard said: "Stay away from Hutch Gainer."

He stepped closer and raised the pipe. My left forearm went up instinctively and I threw a straight right, which caught him on the chin. He took two steps back. Then someone grabbed my right arm and yanked it back. I pulled down to free it, then swung my elbow wildly behind and felt it strike something solid—possibly a skull. I heard a grunt.

Then the numbers caught up with me.

A gun was in my ear.

"Weren't told to kill you," a high-pitched voice said. The dull scent of sweat wafted. "But if we have to, we will. Like the man said, stay away from Hutch Gainer."

Beard stood before me now, his nose bleeding. "Let it go, man."

Then something—probably the butt of the gun—exploded against the back of my head. And everything went dark.

# Chapter Six

——

A FRIEND OF MINE, following a near-fatal accident, had said he'd seen a tunnel and a light. But in my silent and dark state, my dreams were fragmented and unclear. Many were of Lisa Trembley; the others were of golf. In one, Lisa wore a wedding gown but had replaced the veil with her headset, and asked questions I would not answer.

Then, through blurred vision, I saw the bright light. It appeared amid patches of gray, like a movie dream, and things slowly came into focus.

I awoke.

When I saw Perkins in the chair beside me, I knew I hadn't died. His hair was still more white than blond; his eyes more teal than green. He was six-foot-five, 275 pounds, with the same size waist as my 36 inches.

"Sleeping beauty awakes," he said and set a copy of *Soldier of Fortune* on the floor beside his armchair. He shook his head. "How do you get yourself in these messes?" He wore a plain white Izod shirt, jeans, running shoes, and a shoulder holster. A dark blue windbreaker hung from his chair. His feet were crossed at the ankles and rested on a metal bar on the side of my bed.

"Tim Silver just left," he said. "He hasn't changed a bit—told me I had great biceps. Does he talk like that to the other caddies?"

I shook my head, but didn't speak. I was trying to take everything in. The words seemed to come at me too quickly.

"Lisa's been here, too," he said, "with some of your things. She

——

43

wanted to stay, but I sent her home. She's a good one. Probably too good for you. She told me, if you woke up before she got back, to kiss you for her. But we both know that ain't happening."

It was a hospital room: white bare walls, ceramic gray floor, and a TV near the ceiling on which a muted hockey game played. The room's other bed was made and empty. Outside, it was bright. And the ceiling light felt like a flashlight beam on my eyes.

"There's a couple guys been waiting for you to wake up," he said. "A PGA Tour security guy and a local cop."

"We still in Houston?"

"Tucson."

"That's what I meant."

"Sure. You've been in and out for a while. You made the cut, but withdrew."

I didn't speak.

"Know what happened?"

"Yeah," I said. "Who won?"

"Els is leading. Another round to go. Want to tell me what the hell happened?"

"When did you get here?"

"Six hours after Lisa called. Friday about four A.M."

"You should be home with Linda and Jackie."

He shook his head. "I'm here and staying."

"It was a warning."

"You remember everything?"

"I think so," I said.

"Tell me."

"You've been watching golf on TV?"

"Only when infomercials aren't on."

"Heard of Hutch Gainer?"

"The rookie?"

"Yeah." I began with Hutch's on-course remarks, moved to his midnight visit, told Perkins of Pickorino and Kiko, and concluded with Hutch's locker-room dash and my warning.

When I was finished, he said: "You just described a professional hit—surround and converge."

Abruptly two men entered, carrying three Styrofoam cups with plastic lids. The one in the navy blue suit handed a coffee to Perkins and remained standing. It was Tom Schilling, head of PGA Tour Security. Schilling wore a red tie with blue diamonds which had a shoddy knot. You can tell a lot about a guy by his tie knot. Schilling hadn't taken the time to make a Windsor. His was the once-around-up-and-through, the half triangle you see hanging at half-mast on drunks.

Schilling had come aboard about the time Tigermania began. As the world grew more and more violent and full of crazies, and golfers continued to walk defenselessly among throngs of fans, the Tour decided to take precaution. Schilling was a former FBI man, maybe 40, with blow-dried blond hair, perfect fingernails, and a deep tan.

The other man sat beside Perkins in a straight chair and pulled the plastic lid off his Styrofoam cup. He shifted in his seat and looked uncomfortable in his powder-blue shirt, gray tie, and dark blue blazer; he wore light blue slacks that tried to match the shirt but failed. Perkins had said the man was a Tucson cop and I guessed he was more accustomed to a uniform. He had neatly cut, thick, black hair, a moustache, and dark skin.

"I'm Mike Chee," the cop said. "How're you feeling?"

"Ready for the back nine."

He smiled genuinely.

"Jack," Schilling said, "Tom Schilling, Tour Security." He extended a hand.

We had met previously, but Schilling was the type who would forget. The movement to shake his hand made my right side scream. I had to have bruised or cracked ribs.

"Looks like that hurts," Schilling said.

"Bruised ribs hurt like hell," Perkins said. "Ever have one?"

"I was in the FBI. What do you think?"

"Ever have one?" Perkins said again.

Schilling glared at him, then said to me: "Just rest, Jack. The doctor report lists two black eyes, a broken nose..."

"The mirror's not going to be friendly," Perkins said to me.

"... a bruised forearm, and a deeply bruised rib."

When my lights had gone out, Beard and friends must have continued their party. It didn't speak well for the resort community police patrol.

"Who's running the investigation?" I said.

Perkins chuckled.

"I am," Chee said. "We just," he looked Schilling in the eye, "worked that out." His gaze returned to me. "My superiors don't think much of a high-profile guy being—" he searched for the word and shrugged as if settling on one he didn't like—"mugged. A PGA Tour event is supposed to attract tourists. Gila big-shots are so upset, the Gila private force bucked it over to us in Tucson."

"Portray the area in a good light," I said.

"Yeah," he said. "No one wants people scared away. So my boss wants me to get to the bottom of this."

Perkins smiled and sipped his coffee.

"Mr. Schilling will be involved in everything, but this is not strictly a golf matter."

Schilling pressed on. "We want to know all you can remember. Several witnesses said four men wearing sunglasses, moving too fast to recognize, chased you through a coffee shop, into a back alley."

"Never heard of a mugging that sounded like that," Chee said and I saw something in his eyes that fell between suspicion and doubt.

Outside, the sun was bright. My eyes were adjusting to the light. My head still ached, but I remembered everything: the chase, the thugs, and the warning.

I turned back to Schilling. "I can't remember a thing."

"Nothing?" Schilling said.

"I'm exhausted. I need a nap."

*　*　*

"Why lie to them?" Perkins said when I had woken. "Why not tell them what you told me?"

Fire ran up and down my side when I shifted in bed to face him. I took a slow breath.

He was sitting in the leather chair, his feet propped on the extension, hands folded quietly in his lap.

"Chee's a local cop," he said. "Yeah, Schilling's a twerp, but Chee could help. He'd know who the local talent is."

"I don't think they were local," I said.

Outside, the setting sun made a long fire-orange band across a distant mesa. It was late afternoon; the tourney was probably over or in extra holes.

"Who won the tournament?" I said.

"Ernie Els."

I nodded.

He reached for the lever on the chair's side, put both feet on the floor, and leaned forward. "What exactly have you gotten yourself into, Jack?"

Someone knocked at the door and a woman's voice said: "Mr. Perkins, I'm coming in."

The industrial-strength door slowly opened and a large-boned black woman with long hair peeked in. A broad smile crossed her face as she entered. "Dinner time, Jack. I like to warn your friend. The first night, his gun was out when I walked in."

Perkins spread his hands. She set the tray in front of me and left. It was meatloaf, but if food hadn't been an integral part of my life, I wouldn't have known.

"More leather meatloaf," Perkins said.

"You've been eating here?"

"I haven't left this room."

"You knew it wasn't a mugging?"

"I know you better than that," he said. "Got the piece I'm wearing, and my little .22 taped to the back of the toilet. You said they gave you a warning, Jack. Next time might be for real."

I didn't say anything.

"There going to be a next time, Jack?"

"What do you mean?"

"You going to keep pushing?"

The TV near the ceiling was still on; ESPN's *Sports Center* was muted, but over the anchor's shoulder, I saw my face, then a highlight of me hitting a shot. I scrambled for the remote on the metal bed rail and hit the volume: "...Austin remains hospitalized near Tucson. Tour officials and local authorities are still looking into the matter." Then, on the screen, Chee saying: "We're concerned because it doesn't appear to be a random mugging." Then Schilling: "It appears Mr. Austin was simply in the wrong place at the wrong time."

I shook my head. "Glad they agree on the circumstances."

Perkins smiled.

"Tour wants to keep it under wraps," I said.

I closed my eyes. Perkins was still waiting for an answer to his question. Neither the guns nor his presence surprised me. Before he'd played for the New England Patriots and gone on to law enforcement, we had grown up as next-door neighbors and best friends. One story defines him: his sister married a drunk who beat her once. The guy spent two months in the hospital following what was assumed a hit-and-run. The drunk said he couldn't remember what had happened, but when he got out, he packed, accepted his wife's divorce terms, and left town without a word. Perkins never mentioned it, but the night of the so-called hit-and-run, he had returned to our dorm room late, with a soiled shirt and blood on the backs of his hands.

And I, too, was considered family.

"You going to keep pushing?" he said again.

I opened my eyes and found him staring at me, so I adjusted the bed to sit up. The movement made me grunt.

"That feel good?" he grinned.

I gave him the finger.

"Twerp or not," he said. "Schilling is Tour Security and should probably know."

"Think of what happens if the media gets wind of this," I said. "A Tour pro throwing strokes?"

"Scandal."

"More than that," I said.

"Humiliation for Gainer? He deserves it."

"He does deserve it," I said. "But the game doesn't. Right now we get 160,000 spectators at The Players Championship. The game's more popular than baseball."

"Jesus," he said, "golf as our national pastime."

"I'm serious," I said. "If it doesn't end here, where will it end? This is a seven-hundred-million-dollar industry."

"So you're helping Hutch Gainer?"

"The game," I said. "Not Hutch. Look what it's given me."

He took the fork off my tray and tried the meatloaf. He did not drop to the floor, clutching his throat.

"Be easier," he said chewing, "to just tell Pickorino and let him take Gainer out."

"You could do that, couldn't you?"

"Hey," he said and spread his hands.

"Then we'd never find out where the blackmail was coming from," I said, "and it could go on and on."

"And what do we do when we find out? And suppose Pickorino's the blackmailer. Then what?"

To that, I had no answer, so I took the fork from him and ate my meatloaf. He was right: it did taste like leather.

\* \* \*

It was Monday at 3:12 A.M. and Perkins was sleeping in the chair when I woke. He had begun the night in the room's empty bed; I hadn't heard him move to the chair. I picked up the copy of *King Lear*. The lines I usually enjoyed most were those by Fool, but tonight I thought of my warning and the guns, which seemed strewn throughout the room, and I related to Lear's role—a man who should've known better.

Shortly after 5:00, the heavy door to my room pushed open, waking me again. I stirred—my book open on my chest—and rolled slowly to my side, the pain inserting an instant alertness.

In the chair, Perkins sat up, his right hand on the butt of the pistol in the shoulder holster.

A small man entered wearing a white coat and carrying a clipboard.

Perkins dropped his hand to his side. "Doc," he said.

"Hello, Mr. Perkins. Most of our visitors do not wear guns."

"You've seen my license, Doc," Perkins said.

"And I still disapprove." He approached my bed, and immediately shook my hand; the stretch made me cringe.

"Just testing," he said. "You're very big and strong, but that rib will take some time to heal. I'm Dr. Stan Johnson. Your friend, Mr. Perkins, has been here the whole time"—his eyes went to Perkins—"with his gun."

Still seated with his hands clasped behind his head, Perkins sat smirking.

"We'll be sending you home soon," the doctor said, "but you'll be sore a while."

"How long are we talking?"

"That depends. I think you'll be playing in roughly a month."

"That's the earliest?" I asked.

Johnson crossed his arms. "You've got an injured rib. Playing will not allow it to heal. You were beaten." His gaze went to Perkins. "Not difficult to understand, given the company you keep."

Perkins winked at him.

"What's the *soonest* I could play golf?" I said. "Give me something to shoot for."

The doctor sighed and rubbed his chin. "Want a goal? Three weeks. But don't count on it. Relax, rest, and let time take its course."

"Sure."

"I'll be in later to check on you."

Perkins gave a two-finger salute.

Johnson ignored that and left.

I said to Perkins: "That guy *hates* you."

"Yeah, he called the cops when I arrived. You slept through the whole thing, but it was quite a show—resort police, guns drawn, the whole bit."

"Shoot it out on the coronary ward?"

"Nah, I get along pretty good with Chee," he said.

Outside, the sun was rising in dramatic fashion, typical of the Southwest, appearing over the Rincon Mountains, cutting a teal strip through the night's blackness and highlighting the moon. Tucson is surrounded by four mountain ranges: the Santa Catalinas to the north; the Rincons to the east; the Santa Ritas to the south; and the Tucson Mountains to the west. Although I would prefer to have not been locked up in a hospital, at least the view was fabulous. I watched the sunrise, then went back to sleep, as Perkins began his morning ritual of push-ups and sit-ups.

# Chapter Seven

———

THE NEXT TIME I opened my eyes, Lisa was sitting on the edge of the bed, holding my hand. Silver was sitting in Perkins's chair. I heard the shower running, then stop. I didn't notice what Silver had on, but Lisa wore formfitting jeans, a cream-colored sweater set, and her hair was pulled back and somehow stayed atop her head. She had on large gold hoop earrings and a gold chain I'd given her for Valentine's Day.

"I love you." She ran a hand through my hair and touched the side of my face, then began to cry. "God, you look awful."

"Thanks."

She leaned forward and hugged me.

The bathroom door opened and Perkins walked out, the sleeves of a white MASSACHUSETTS POLICE ACADAMY T-shirt stretched taut over his arms.

"You've got fantastic biceps," Silver said.

Lisa chuckled into my chest. I grinned.

"Jesus Christ," Perkins said. "Stop hitting on me. I'm married."

Lisa glanced up at me and I kissed her. It was a long, hard kiss. We stayed like that.

"Christ," Perkins said. "I'll be in the hall. I need something to eat anyway. Silver, you going to stay and watch that?"

"You asking me to breakfast, Rambo?" Silver said.

"Sure. Whatever. Go down and get it. I'll buy."

"What a sweetie."

"Cut that shit out."

I heard the door shut behind them.

When we broke, Lisa slid onto the bed beside me, atop the covers, and we lay like that, holding hands. The jarring of the mattress hurt my side, and made me wonder why the kiss hadn't.

"We've got so much to talk about," she said. "I'll get to the bottom of this. CBS brass has already given me the green light."

"Green light?"

"To begin an investigative report," she said. "Tom Schilling said you told him you don't remember much. What do you remember now?" Her head propped in her hand, she lay smiling. When her bangs fell in her face, she brushed them away absently.

I was getting a headache. I loved this woman. Yet, I couldn't tell her about Hutch Gainer. She would dive right into the middle of things. My mind raced: Lisa, Hutch, the Tour, my stubbornness. I had always been single-minded, a man of black and white, right and wrong, typical of those who battle dyslexia. That doggedness had allowed me to turn my slightly above-average ability into a PGA Tour career. Now that same determination had me in a position to deceive my future wife. Once again, I thought of my father and the beliefs I shared with him. I hated what Hutch Gainer had done. He had committed acts, which, if publicized, could leave fans questioning every failed shot. Yet, if someone didn't stop this stroke-throwing scandal now, where would it end?

Still holding my hand, Lisa reached up and touched my cheek. "Does that hurt?"

I shook my head.

"I spoke with the doctor," she said, "who's very nice by the way. He said you don't have amnesia. So you should remember what happened."

I looked at her blankly.

"Detective Chee, with the Tucson PD, said you were chased into a coffee shop. You remember that, right?"

"Huh?"

"The coffee shop. You remember being chased inside, of course."

I smiled weakly. She'd already assigned herself to the story and begun the interviews.

"I tracked down some people who were in the coffee shop at the time," she said. "A girl told me four men dressed similarly chased you inside and out the back. That would all be consistent with Chee's report."

"Am I just another story to you?" I smiled.

She had no time for jokes. "The crime scene technician said he found nothing. But they're still looking for clues."

"You've already talked to the crime scene technician?"

"Of course."

My headache was getting worse.

"I thought you were a golf analyst?"

"That's not funny. You know I'm a journalist who loves golf."

"NCAA Women's Champ in 1985," I said.

"Jack, some professionals I've spoken with say some thoughts might be repressed, but they are significant and should be dealt with."

"What?"

She repeated the whole thing.

"Shrinks?"

"Yes, Sweetie." She squeezed my hand. "I've been working on this, Honey. I'm taking vacation time to be with you."

"You've talked to shrinks, cops, the doctor, a kid in the coffee shop—"

"I'm meeting with her again this afternoon."

"Wonderful," I said.

She let go of my hand. "What do you mean by 'wonderful'?"

The TV was not on and the hallway was silent. The quiet was almost tangible. I had figured Lisa would want to cover my accident, even push until she found something. But I had also figured I would have time to prepare—a gross miscalculation.

"Jack, I've been busting my butt, trying to help. Chee said it doesn't look like a mugging. He said it looks very suspicious. Frankly, I agree. Four guys dressed to hide their appearance chase you into an alley, then beat you?"

Christ, she was smart. She had started at the *Washington Post*, which doesn't hire reporters who can't chase—and catch—a story.

"There's no need for all this concern," I said.

She slid out of bed and sat in the chair and smiled.

I smiled back.

Hers vanished. "What the hell is going on?"

Lisa swore about as often as John Daly lays up on a par five.

"I spoke to three psychologists. All agreed you should remember at least scattered images. You didn't suffer brain damage, Jack."

I sat staring. Brain damaged or not, I was beginning to feel dazed. My future was with this woman, not Hutch Gainer. "O.K.," I said. "I won't lie to you. There's something going on, which doesn't really involve me. I can't tell you what it is."

"You've been beaten up, Jack. Does it involve the Tour?"

I was silent.

"I've been on the streets of DC. I've been to the jungles of South America. Been knocked down and punched. One guy tried to rape me. I can handle myself, Jack Austin. Tell me."

I don't claim to be the smartest guy in the word, certainly not smart enough to understand women. But I knew I didn't want to lose her. I didn't want her to leave angry. Yet I couldn't tip my hand.

She waited.

"That's all I can say, Lisa."

She had her small index finger pointed sternly at me, the skin pulled tight over her cheeks, her mouth opened to speak. That was when the door opened and Silver walked in. My relief bordered on ecstasy—until I saw who was behind him: Hutch Gainer, John Pickorino, Kiko, and the blonde.

* * *

They entered in single file behind Silver: Kiko, looking petulant, a bully who'd met his match; the blonde, dressed for show, moving with her head down as if bored; Hutch, walking slowly, knowing full well the gravity of it all; then Pickorino, dressed in a navy blue suit, padding with ease, smiling as if amused.

Perkins followed them, his gun drawn but very discreetly in the palm of his hand. Someone else's—I presumed Kiko's—was in his belt.

Lisa stood wide-eyed, amazed at the spectacle. She went to her purse, found a pen and pad and held them at her sides, ever ready. Silver walked over and stood next to her.

Pickorino glanced at Lisa's hands. He nodded to himself, then looked her over, removing the rectangular glasses. Finally, he approached my bedside. The dark suit seemed to set off his white hair and added a distinguished quality, which I knew would go well with his diction and the rhythmic meter of his syntax.

"We have come to wish you well," he said. "Your friend is not a trusting type."

I didn't like what Hutch had done to Pickorino, but I had been beaten and this guy may very well have ordered it.

Hutch had on a jean shirt, ironed and creased blue jeans, black boots, and held his Stetson hat at his side. When we made eye contact he smiled. Nothing unusual here, just two Tour buddies sharing a moment—in no way was he responsible for me lying in a hospital bed with a face like a Halloween mask. Kiko glared at Perkins. The blonde had on a white fur coat that must've cost 50 animals their lives. She wore it open, over a low-cut party dress, which fit the way a leather miniskirt should. She had on spiked heels and pearls. Her hair was big, teased on top.

When my eyes hit on her hands, they stopped.

The first two fingernails of her right hand were the color of a plum and contrasted greatly with the rest of her manicured and painted nails. The fingers were red with burst blood vessels and deeply bruised.

She was eyeing Lisa with a gaze that fell between outright disapproval and a form of jealousy I'd seen only among women.

Perkins leaned on the wall to my right, gun still drawn.

"How are you feeling, Jack?" Pickorino said.

"You know anything about the hit?" I said. Behind Pickorino, Lisa's eyes leaped into fifth gear, and instantly I regretted the question.

She raised her pen to the pad, looked uneasily about, and waited.

"Is that what this is about?" Pickorino looked dejectedly at Kiko. "Kiko, my friend, Mr. Austin does not understand how we do business." He stopped short, then to Silver and Lisa, he said: "Would you excuse us? I would care to chat with Jack and his large friend here alone."

Silver started for the door. Lisa said, "I'm his fiancée. I stay."

"Lisa," I said, "it'll just be a moment."

"What the hell's going on?"

"*Lisa*," I said.

Her eyes ran to Perkins. His gaze was flat and dull, as if watching a boring movie.

"Tell me," I said.

"Sorry," he said.

She looked at me again. "Damn it. I'll get to the bottom of this." She stormed out.

Pickorino said: "Jenna, would you care to get us coffee?"

"I don't want coffee," Jenna said.

"Jenna, that was not a request."

"He's your glory boy." She pointed to Hutch. "Have him go."

"You are mine also," Pickorino said. "And I asked *you*."

"I'm not yours," Jenna said.

"You will get the coffee or..." Pickorino eyed her hand with raised brows.

Her eyes followed his to her bruised hand. She looked up at him and tried to hold his stare. She couldn't. She turned and went out.

Hutch moved toward the door after Jenna.

"No, Hutch," Pickorino said, "you stay. This is family business. You are family."

Hutch just bobbed his head, then sat in a straight chair on the far wall. Kiko walked to the window, admired the view, then moved to the side of my bed, opposite Pickorino. He stood several feet from Perkins, looking down at me, shaking his head.

"Honey of a girl you got there," he said. "Great ass and some attitude. Probably great in the sack—"

Perkins hit him on the chin with a straight left, and was back leaning against wall before anyone knew what happened. Kiko's jaw snapped toward his right shoulder. He went down and was out cold on the floor.

"Should respect a man's future wife," Perkins said.

Pickorino moved to the end of the bed, looked down at Kiko, and rubbed his chin. Then he glanced at Perkins more amused than ever. "You are very good. Kiko needs to learn respect. However, he is very vengeful. Beware."

That made Perkins smile.

"We did not," Pickorino said, "come to see how my bodyguard stacks up, Jack. I am here to offer my services. I have been in business a long time and have many connections."

I lay silent, listening. The last thing I expected was an offer from him to help.

"I have made some calls and come up with nothing," Picorino said, "which is very odd. But I will continue to try, and I was prepared to offer Kiko as protection." He grinned at Perkins. "I see now that will be unnecessary."

The room was quiet. I lay, digesting it all and fighting sensory overload.

"Why would you ask if I knew about the hit?" Pickorino said.

"You're a mobster."

"That is a very ugly term."

"It's an ugly business."

"Retail is business, Jack. I dabble. Little of this, little of that. I am president of a multifaceted enterprise."

In the corridor, I could hear some type of cart being wheeled. The antiseptic odor of the room had now given way to the salty scent of sweat. I didn't know if it had been Perkins's short-lived exchange with Kiko, or just the nervous tension, which abounded.

"Jack, I will help you, but I will also warn you: beware of what you say to me. I am a man with many means."

My headache was now in full bloom. It was 8:30 A.M. and it might very well be a migraine by noon.

"Why would you want to help me?" If, indeed, he was responsible for the warning, helping me would easily allow him to monitor my activities and progress—or, whenever he felt ready, to finish the job completely.

On the floor, Kiko made a noise like a grunt.

"Jack, I am an old man. Once I was young, tough, and proud. I have made a great deal of money over the years. It has bought me," he motioned at where the blonde had been, "some happiness. But the companionship of one half my age, who needs to be disciplined so often, is fleeting at best."

I said nothing, but wondered what Pickorino's discipline consisted of. Whatever it was, I wouldn't want to trade places with Jenna.

The amusement was no longer in his eyes. "Do you enjoy the symphony?"

"No," I said.

"Well I do and golf brings me equal happiness. I enjoy playing, but more so, watching professionals play the way brilliant artists perform. I also enjoy watching the competition and struggle to win."

That didn't sound like anyone who'd want to fix the outcome of a round. But business was business and, as he had said, his was multifaceted.

"I am a fan of golf, and felt I might have something to offer." He stared penetratingly at me. "I was raised in an orphanage. I have done many things of which I'm not proud. At my age, one tends to look back over his life. I will make good for my wrongdoings my own way. This is one way."

"No thanks."

His eyes flickered—open and shut once—with insult. Then he looked angry.

Kiko made more noise, then climbed to his feet. "Cheap shot, sonofabitch," he said to Perkins.

"There are no cheap shots in life," Pickorino said. "You must be ready at all times. Jack, I see that you are uneasy. Very understandable. I will, however, continue to look into this. Should I come up with anything, I will let you know."

He walked out and the others followed. Before leaving, Hutch paused and I glared at him.

Perkins followed them and returned several minutes later.

I was rubbing my temples. "Walk them to the elevator?"

"Yeah. Lisa and Silver left."

"If Lisa wasn't enough, Pickorino thinks he's Ken Starr investigating this."

"Maybe he wants to become a reporter," Perkins said. "They weren't here to try anything. Had the girl with them."

"I don't think Pickorino cares much what happens to Jenna."

"On a first-name basis with her?"

"You saw her hand," I said.

"There's nothing we can do about it."

A cart rolled down the hall again.

"All I'm saying," Perkins said, "is they wouldn't do anything in front of her. She'd be a witness, and the old man must know she'd sell him out for another fur coat."

"True," I said. "And his offer to help doesn't mean he didn't order the hit."

# Chapter Eight

——

ON MONDAY, PERKINS WATCHED ESPN from the morning exercise shows to late-night Sports Center, which updated my condition and the status of the case—stating, in effect, that no one knew a thing.

After dinner, I sat near the window in the fading sunlight and continued slowly with *King Lear*. I had reached the scene where Lear's daughter orders Gloucester's eyes removed so he can no longer see the truth, when Tom Schilling showed up with Detective Mike Chee again. Chee carried himself like one who had been around the block a few times, and seemed to be a stand-up guy. Schilling, on the other hand, was the kind of guy who'd hit on somebody's wife.

On this evening, Schilling's blow-dried hair was tornado proof, and I could smell expensive cologne. In fairness, the cologne could've been Chee's, but if it was, it had cost more than his entire ensemble: a polyester navy blue sports coat, gray slacks that were a little short, cordovan loafers, black dress socks, and a navy tie.

Chee gave an easy smile, and shook my hand. "The side seems better. Last time we shook, you flinched."

"Thanks," I said. "A little better every day." I didn't have the heart to point out the socks clashed with the tie.

"Jack," Schilling said, "you have anything more to offer since we last spoke?"

I shook my head. Perkins was in the straight chair and I remained in the recliner near the window. They stood across the room.

——

"That's interesting," Schilling said. "Bunch of doctors say you should remember."

"Sorry."

"Padre Tarbuck said your jokes were bad but you were very bright and you could probably help."

"I wish I could."

"Your fiancée's driving me bananas. Acts like I don't know what I'm doing."

I nearly said, *Imagine that*, but didn't.

"Had to inform her I worked for the FBI."

"Use that line often?" I said.

Schilling shot me his tough-guy glare. It told me why he was no longer with the Bureau. "Look," he said, "we've gone through that alley with a comb. There's nothing there."

"You've done all you could. I appreciate the effort."

"But," Schilling held up a finger for me to wait, "out of the blue, Lisa comes into my office and asks if there's ever been any documented Mafia activity around the Tour."

I nearly swallowed my tongue.

Schilling folded his arms across his chest. "Not sure what to make of that."

Lisa hadn't mentioned Pickorino's visit since she'd stormed out of my room. She'd come in with gifts—magazines, newspapers, even a new *Complete Works of Shakespeare* to replace my tattered edition—and had chatted about the wedding. I should've been suspicious, but it's hard to be on your toes when the highlight of your day is your next nap.

"She's been to see you, too?" I said to Chee.

"Ms. Trembley? Yeah," he said, "a very competent reporter—most aren't. She's impressive."

"What'd she ask?" I said.

Chee nodded. "Mafia—in Tucson to be specific."

Perkins, taking it all in, stood and walked across the room, stretching his legs.

"Jack," Schilling said, "got anything you'd like to tell us?"

"In reference to what?"

"The hell do you think?"

"I don't know what she's doing. We're supposed to get married this summer. She's got a lot on her mind."

"She said three guys and a woman came to see you. That they were absolute mobsters."

"Is an 'absolute mobster' more criminal than just a plain mobster?"

"Want to tell us about the visit?" Schilling took out a small pad and pen and prepared to scrawl.

"Did you know Shakespeare's Globe Theater was formed in 1600?"

"You know something, Jack?" Schilling said. "I think you're up to your ears in shit."

"The proverbial buried lie."

"You don't cooperate with us, you're going to get burned."

Daylight had faded. From the hallway, I heard voices and a cacophony to which I was accustomed. My days had been long and dull; Schilling's threat would probably be my excitement for the week.

"A lot of people have come to see me," I said. "I don't remember everyone, but certainly no one who's involved in organized criminal activity." I sounded like a college professor lecturing. *The Art of the Evasive Interview*, Journalism 101 with Dr. Austin.

"Tom," Chee said, "we're not going to get anything. Let's go."

"We're offering to help," Schilling said.

"I don't know what you're talking about," I said. "Lisa's under a great deal of stress. She wants answers that aren't there." I spread my hands. "Wrong place at the wrong time."

Chee forced a smile.

Schilling stood staring. "Wrong place at the wrong time, huh?"

"Yes."

They moved to the door and Chee went out. Schilling turned back. "Whatever you're involved in," he said, "it's not too late to step out of it."

"Just the wrong place at the wrong time."

Schilling shook his head slowly and went out.

Perkins began doing handstand push-ups, leaning against the far wall.

From his inverted position, he said: "Looks to me like the cat's out of the bag."

His voice had all the strain of a guy sipping espresso, maybe reading *US* magazine in some café in Paris. I mused on Perkins wearing a beret, holding the tiny cup, his little finger extended. It made me smile.

"Come here from the snow and don't even get outside," I said. "Why don't you go for a run?"

"Don't want to get chased into an alley and beaten up."

"Cute."

"Being locked up in here gives us a chance to think,"he said." You come up with anything yet?"

I hadn't. I moved from the recliner back to bed. The room had been showered with flowers—nearly every guy on Tour (or his wife or girlfriend) had sent a bouquet.

On my food tray, the phone rang.

"Jack?"

I knew the small voice and Texas accent. "Yeah, Hutch."

Perkins got to his feet.

"Jack, like, I wanted to apologize."

"Listen," I said, "the guy who was here, Perkins, has agreed to take the case. He's a PI and you're paying him—" I covered the receiver and waited.

"Six hundred a day, plus expenses."

I raised my brows.

"I'm good," he said.

I relayed the terms to Hutch.

"I'll pay anything," Hutch said. "I missed another cut."

"No way you could've made it. What's Pickorino doing?"

"He's really fixed on helping you. He's, like, calling around, asking people, even cops."

"Might be an act," I said. "Might be the one behind the whole thing."

Hutch was silent, as if he hadn't considered that before. It made me wonder. I knew he wasn't brilliant, no candidate for an aeronautical engineering degree, but the guy had to possess some common sense.

"He's, like, too serious about trying to find out who beat you up. I mean, like, since we left your room, he's been on the phone."

I didn't say anything.

"Jack," he said, "I don't know how much more I can take. Walking into the locker room everyday, seeing the guys—"

I had nothing to offer.

"There's no way out of this," Hutch said. His voice was becoming urgent, as if he were making realizations. "I'm trapped. As long as Pickorino's around, whoever it is can keep blackmailing me."

"Pickorino's just a means to an end," I said. "Whoever it is would find something on someone else to use."

"But it wouldn't be me."

"Nice attitude."

"It *wouldn't* be me."

"Hutch, I'm not looking out for you. Where I come from, you appreciate what you've been given. And I've been given a hell of a lot."

"When is your friend going to start?"

"Are you listening?"

"He's here," Hutch blurted. Then the connection broke.

I set the phone on the receiver, leaned back against my pillow.

"Well?" Perkins said.

"He called to see when you were going to put on your armor, get on your white horse, and ride out to save his ass."

"Nice analogy."

"He agreed to the terms," I said.

We were quiet. He went back to his workout and boredom. I went back to my convalescing and boredom.

"You know," I said, "Lisa's around and I'm fine. Why don't you go?"

"And leave you sitting here in bed like a duck on a pond?"

"I've got that .22 in the bathroom. Besides, if someone was going to make a run at me they'd have done it before I could talk to the cops. Either they know I won't talk, or now think I don't have anything to tell."

"Or they're waiting to see if you back off." Perkins was doing conventional push-ups now. He clicked on the TV between sets. "If we're talking Mafia, they own the cops anyway. Maybe they assume the hit did enough—scared you into not talking."

"Go home to Linda and Jackie for a couple days, then take on the case."

Outside the room, I heard my nurse's voice. The hospital and my ward were becoming too familiar, the way a person doesn't notice when his air conditioning or furnace rumbles on.

Perkins sat on the windowsill, considering what I'd said.

"I appreciate you coming here on a moment's notice," I said. "But it's time. No one knows you're on the case, so no one knows I'm still pushing."

Perkins considered that. He shook his head, then started to speak.

I cut him off. "This is my mess," I said. "You can't stay with me forever. Go see your family."

# Chapter Nine

———

LISA'S ROCKVILLE, MARYLAND HOME was a stone, two-story colonial that looked like Queen Elizabeth's summer cottage. Of course, to a guy who owned a two-room fishing camp on a lake in northern Maine and a two-bedroom condo near Orlando, every home in Rockville looked majestic. You couldn't buy one for less than four hundred grand.

She had left Tucson before me to get things set and had yet to ask additional questions about my sensitivity session with the four thugs, which I took to be a bad sign. At last contact, Perkins was doing his thing in New Orleans; Silver had put his journalism master's to work and said he was doing something for Lisa's boss at CBS; and I was still doing nothing—not playing golf, not helping Perkins, not even being a pain to Schilling. As if to add insult to my injuries, Rockville had received a rare late-winter snowstorm, leaving me to do what I had done as a boy—stare out windows at the enemy of every golfer located in the Northeast: snow-covered ground.

I had on jeans and a white T-shirt that said POWER BAR, and sat with my feet up in Lisa's living room, tossing a golf ball from hand to hand, staring out the bay window at the neighborhood. Rockville is the kind of place where people drive Land Rovers, kids go to boarding school, and you buy Starbucks to grind at home. Sun reflected off the snow-covered lawn behind Lisa's house. The aroma of something roasting was in the air and we had a fire going. The good life—Land Rovers, Starbucks, and a roaring fire.

I wished I were playing golf.

Her CBS contract allowed her to buy the house. Paintings and photos hung decoratively from the living room walls and the furniture was forest green. Across the room, Lisa sat typing on a laptop. She wore jeans, a huge white sweater, and Big Bunny slippers with ears that stood up straight. It had been a week since I'd been chased into the alley.

I tossed the ball up and fumbled the catch. It clunked on the hardwood floor and rolled noisily.

"Still bored?" she said.

"I'm usually playing this time of year."

"It's good to smell the roses."

On an area carpet in front of the fireplace, I had my Bullseye putter, three Titleists, and a water glass. I got up and nudged the balls into position, six feet from the glass. I took two practice strokes—still sore, but feeling better. I thought of the image: me, white athletic socks on my feet, putting into an empty water glass in the dead of winter. The flashback took me to my childhood during Maine's harshest months. The water glass suddenly became a well-manicured hole. *Austin needs this to win the Masters. Nicklaus is in the clubhouse at 17 under. This putt would set a course record and win by a stroke.* The putt missed.

I walked to Lisa. "Sending an E-mail?"

"Filing a story."

"A story?" I said.

She smiled politely. "I said I'd get to the bottom of this and I will. I'm working from home, going to the local CBS affiliate to tape segments."

"Who's head analyst while you're away?" I said.

"Paul Martin."

She went on typing as if it didn't bother her. I knew better. Martin had been after her job since she'd landed it. She was the only woman serving as head golf analyst for a major network. Martin had just learned to walk upright and said ratings would drop with a woman leading the way. To the contrary, ratings had shot up after Lisa took over. Who would you rather watch— Martin, a 300-pound, out-of-shape ex-golfer who'd never had a prime, or someone who looked like Lisa, and had been the NCAA Women's Champ?

"What about having Martin filling in for you?" I said.

She stopped typing. "I'd be an idiot not to think he was trying everything in his means to get my job." She got up, moved next to me on the couch, and touched my cheek gently, then turned it into a pinch and grinned her wide-eyed, full-of-life smile. "But this face, which I'm about to marry, is my life."

"Thank you."

The phone on the end table rang. I picked it up. "The Trembley home."

"Jack." It was Perkins.

My eyes ran to Lisa. "Sounds like you're in the middle of an interstate," I said.

"Phone booth outside my motel."

"Must be a nice place."

Lisa leaned back, crossed her arms and continued to stare.

"Cut the shit," he said. "Can you talk?"

"No."

"O.K., listen: Stay away from Pickorino. Guy's ruthless. He ice-picked a kid to death over 25 bucks. Temper's legendary. He shows up, do not let him in."

"Very good," I said. "Feeling fine."

Lisa was looking at me.

"Lisa sitting right there?"

"Trying to look into the phone."

She shot me a look, then stood, and went back to the love seat and her typing.

"Second thing: I'm heading to Vegas day after tomorrow. I'll call you from there, but I just got to tell you I've met up with class-A scumbags over the years. Pickorino's at the top of the list."

"I hear you."

"Got the .22 I left?"

"Yeah, Chee pulled strings to get it on the plane."

"I don't care how it got there. Can you fire it?"

"If I have to," I said, "I can."

When I hung up, Lisa continued to type, failing to acknowledge my gaze.

I hit some putts, pushing each one to the right. Simply not concentrating.

"I feel bad," I said, "about this situation."

"You mocked me."

"I—"

"I'm not stupid, Jack. That was Perkins, calling from somewhere, hot on the trail."

I said nothing.

"I'm going to be your wife."

"Yes."

"So you're trying to protect me even though whoever chased you into that alley is involved with the Tour and it's my job to report on it." She smiled politely. "You can stonewall, Jack, but I'm probably closer to figuring things out than you think."

\* \* \*

The walls of the upstairs office were lined with books—from college texts to journalists' accounts of everything. I sat at the desk. The Tour had recently furnished all players with free laptop computers and E-mail accounts.

When I was logged onto the Internet, I punched in www.yahoo.com. When Yahoo came up, I typed "gambling & golf." Research was a skill I should have mastered during college. But golf, pizza, beer, and my 19-year-old hormones had denied me. When the Gamblers Anonymous site came up, I read a list of 20 questions that people were expected to ask themselves. *My name is Jack and I have a problem.* I saved the page to my hard drive, then went back to the search box and typed in "sports gambling." There were plenty of sites. A guy could drop his Visa number and try to make a quick buck—or ruin his life.

I pointed the mouse and clicked on the first site listed. It included a feature article, written by someone with spelling problems. As a dyslexic, I know people who live in glass houses shouldn't throw rocks, but at least I had sense enough to use Spell Check. The feature opened with: "Is sports gambling illegal in the U.S.? What a stupid question, you might think. Of course it is. Maybe it's illegal in the law books. But is it really enforced?" And what followed the intro was what one would expect: although illegal, sports gambling was not enforced, so why not bet online?

Just what the folks at Gamblers Anonymous wanted to hear.

Another site specialized in golf betting. It hadn't been updated since the last Major, but listed the players entered and gave odds on their winning. If someone wanted to bet on weekly Tour events this wasn't the place to do that.

But at the third site I looked at, you could bet on weekly events. I scrolled to my last event. Tiger Woods had good odds. If you put $100 on Woods and he won, the return was $500. I looked for my name. It wasn't listed. I tried to tell myself I enjoyed being the underdog, but after 10 seasons that was wearing thin.

This Internet search didn't answer many questions, but it did provide some information: golf betting was listed right alongside

NFL, NBA, and the other sports where gambling was considered commonplace.

I thought about that: golf could be bet on as easily as football? I didn't like that. I didn't like that at all because I knew full well no sport would be easier to fix; the golf swing is too complex for anyone to be accused of throwing strokes without rock-solid evidence. Or a confession.

\* \* \*

Candles were lit on the dinner table atop white linen. The reflection of the flames danced on the chandelier above the table like sunlight on waves. To go with the roast, Lisa had prepared scallion potatoes, a garden salad, homemade rolls, and glazed carrots. We were both having wine.

She wore a low-cut navy blue dress, dark stockings, and matching heels. I had on a tie, khakis, loafers, and a navy sports jacket. Dressing up after lying in bed for a week made me feel human again. The knot in my tie was a perfect Windsor and, I had to admit, I looked dashing. Of course when Lisa dresses up, no one else exists, so it didn't matter. Her hair was pulled up and worn atop her head, her neck ran to smooth shoulders and she wore a string of pearls.

"If you'd have dressed like that and stood in my hospital room," I said. "I'd have healed sooner."

"Thank you," she said. "I think."

We ate in comfortable silence for a while. When I looked across the table, she was smiling.

"What?" I said. "Food on my chin? This is the first good meal I've had in—"

"You don't have anything on your face. In fact, you look great. I was just thinking about the first time I saw you in the hospital."

"Come a long way in a week?"

"A marathon. How does it feel to be back among the living?"

"Great."

"You know, despite your being a huge pain in the butt—and I mean *huge*—I actually enjoy this."

I sipped some red wine, then stared at the glass. "I love being alone with you. But not under these circumstances. I had some plans for this season."

"Tell me the plans," she said.

"What?"

"Tell me. Go ahead."

"They're just some goals. I make a list before every season and keep it in my wallet. Helps me stay focused."

"Are they private?" She took a tiny piece of lettuce with the tip of her fork and placed it in her mouth.

"Never told anyone about the list before."

"Would you like to share it with me?"

Lisa was my best friend. Perkins was like a brother, but that was different. I wouldn't share the list with him. Still, some items on that list had been in my wallet for the entire decade I'd spent on tour; those goals, having never been accomplished, got repeated year after year with only me knowing them. Now Lisa wanted to see them. She and I had met on Tour, spent all our time together there. However, this was our first real taste of married life, a true trial run. I already knew I wasn't helping the trial any by not telling her all I knew about Hutch Gainer.

She was looking at her plate, chewing.

I removed my wallet, pulled a small tattered sheet of paper from it and handed it to her.

"Jack," she said, "it's O.K. I don't need to see it. You hesitated enough for me to know you're uncomfortable sharing it with me. It must be personal."

"If I had doubts," I said, "I wouldn't be here."

She didn't speak.

"But, I've been single a long time. It's an adjustment—one I'm looking forward to—but an adjustment nonetheless."

She took the sheet. "Win a major; win a Tour event; and finish top-20 in putting."

"Winning will come if my putting improves. "

She stood, set her cloth napkin down, came around the table, and kissed me. The kiss was long and hard. When we broke, she said nothing, but turned and left the room. She returned to my side moments later, holding her purse, and retrieved her wallet. She handed it to me. "Look inside." She sat across from me again.

I unsnapped the wallet and folded it open. On a browned piece of a paper, in smeared ink, written in Lisa's flowing hand:

1. *work at a major paper*
2. *make a name*
3. *get into sports when I've proved myself as a journalist*
4. *get back to golf*

I looked up from the list and she was grinning. "Two peas in a pod," she said.

"Two peas in a pod—except your goals are accomplished."

We went on eating and were quiet. Then I heard her chair move.

When she got to me, she put a hand on each side of my face and pressed her mouth against mine. This kiss was different from the others I'd received since being injured. There was something in it which was unmistakable. Slowly, I stood and put my arms around her. I unzipped the back of her dress and it slid down her body.

We never made it to the upstairs bedroom.

Afterward, we lay on the floor before the fire, beneath a quilt, holding hands. The flames were lively, casting shadows upon us. Lisa's head was on my chest, and she looked up at me; her dark eyes seemed to shimmer amid the flame's light.

"I love you," I said.

"I love you, too, Pain in the Butt."

# Chapter Ten

———

WITH LISA WORKING from a CBS affiliate in DC, taping segments to be shown during weekend golf coverage, I got up each morning with her. By nature, I woke early; moreover, who could sleep knowing she was hard at work? My ribs were feeling better and I was doing some push-ups. In hotel rooms at night, I'd grown accustomed to doing 200; now three sets of 25 led to exhaustion.

I got out of bed, pulled on jeans and a T-shirt, and went downstairs where I slipped on sneakers and grabbed a fleece-lined jacket with a sponsor's logo on the breast. Late winter in Washington, DC is not late winter in Washington State, but a form of winter nonetheless and the air was far beyond crisp. Tiny clouds of breath appeared as I scuttled down the driveway, past Lisa's white Ford Explorer for the morning paper, my sock-less feet, inside hastily chosen Nikes, crunched the frozen snow-covered driveway. The sound was refreshing; it wasn't soft carpet, hardwood floors, or hospital tile. It felt good to be outside.

So I kept walking. I turned at the bottom of the driveway and walked down the street. The blood flowed easily; my body warmed. I wasn't ready to run, but I was getting better.

At the end of the street—the distance of a good par five—I paused. No one was around, so I put my hands on my hips, bent forward, and made a smooth rotation of the shoulders, as if swinging a club. Sore but not painful. Encouragement can be priceless. I headed back. At the bottom of the driveway, I stood for a moment and scanned the paper's sports section.

———

Now a dark blue Crown Victoria idled, maybe 50 yards away, facing me. Smoke puffed from the exhaust and I saw a silhouette through the windshield. I waved at the driver. The car shifted into gear and drove past me. No time for chitchat in DC's rat race. As quaint as the big-money DC pols had made it, there was no Maine charm in Rockville. But I wouldn't tell Lisa that.

\* \* \*

Inside, I set the *Post* on the table, got a cup of coffee, and went up to the master bedroom. The air upstairs was thick with shower steam, the windows fogged. Lisa stood before a full-length mirror in a black skirt, matching stockings and heels, and only a bra. She was holding a white blouse in front of her and examining the effect in the mirror.

"Conservative," I said.

She turned around and smiled. "Playing in the snow?"

"See me?" I kissed her.

"Just making sure you're all right."

"I'm a big boy, Lis."

"You're recovering."

"Your neighbor's got the personality of a thumbtack."

"Not my neighbor."

"The blue Ford?"

She shook her head.

"Should've known," I said. "Probably a misdemeanor to drive anything but an import here."

"I don't drive an import."

"Rebel."

She smiled.

A strange car in front of Lisa's house at 6:30 A.M.? A week after I'd been warned? And he drove off when I waved? Had I surprised him by going outside?

Or was I overreacting? Maybe the guy pulled to the side to drink his Starbucks.

"Got to put on my face," she said.

"You don't need makeup."

"You, my friend, are blinded by love."

"Or lust."

She patted my side. "We've got to be careful. No more episodes like last night."

"Love heals," I said.

"But lovemaking does not." She went into the bathroom.

I dropped into the push-up position and did 25. If anyone had seen them I'd have been embarrassed to admit I was a professional athlete. There was a twinge of pain in my side, but my shoulders felt warm with the blood flow. After the third set, I stood up feeling as if I'd run a marathon, but feeling good.

I moved to the window and looked out again. The blue car had not returned.

\* \* \*

Lisa was still upstairs getting dressed when Tim Silver showed up with Padre Tarbuck. My injuries had brought Silver's caddying career—or rather the research he was conducting for a book about life on Tour—to an end, at least temporarily. Padre was dressed like an off-duty golfer in khakis and a golf shirt; however, Silver wore a tie. I led them to the living room, where I had been drinking my fourth cup of coffee, watching *Live! with Regis and Kelly*. Realizing what morning TV offered made me appreciate Shakespeare more.

In the living room, Silver shook his head. "For a guy who went to that Shakespeare festival, you got bad taste. You're going to watch daytime TV, check out my man *Montel*. That smile and those buns? He's worth sitting in front of the tube for."

"I'm sure," I said. "Usually I'm on the range by seven."

"You need to rest, Jack," Padre said.

Regis started squealing about something.

Silver shook his head. "I don't know if you need rest bad enough to sit through this."

Padre said: "I flew up yesterday, saw Tim in the airport. We drove over together."

"Thanks for coming."

"I was taking this week off anyway," Padre said. "I should've made it to the hospital. One of the good things about traveling 30 weeks a year: frequent-flyer miles."

I sipped my coffee. "Give me a hand with something?"

We walked to the carpeted dining room, where I had some balls, a glass on its side, and my putter.

I grabbed the putter. "My stroke was just coming around. Don't want to lose that momentum."

"What do you need?" Padre said.

"Yesterday, I was pushing everything to the right."

"Hit a couple," Padre said. "I'll tell you what I see."

I stood about eight feet from the glass and rolled three balls;

the first clinked the back of the cup, but the others both missed right.

"Bringing the putter back outside, then pulling it in. Looks like Billy Mayfair's stroke."

"Cutting across it?"

"Yeah," Padre said.

"Thanks. I'll put a string on the floor and work the putter back and forth, in a straight line. Get that kink out."

"How's married life treating you?" Silver said, walking to the window. "A big adjustment—living together."

I sat in a straight-back chair at the dining room table. Padre joined me.

"This is still the honeymoon," I said.

"I still have trouble believing you're getting hitched," Silver said.

"Heartbroken?"

"Tall, honky, and handsome." He shook his head. "Not my type."

"Racist."

He laughed.

I finished my coffee.

"You've been alone a long time," Silver said. "Just you and golf. It'll be different."

"Different and better," I said.

"I think it's great, Jack," Padre said. "Holy matrimony is a high testament to the Lord."

"Then why aren't you married?" I said.

"I don't have a Lisa."

"Wish I had someone who looked like you, Padre, but acted like Lisa," Silver said.

Padre shook his head. I laughed.

* * *

A short time later, we were in the living room drinking coffee. Silver had channel surfed and ended up where we'd begun, at *Regis*. Through the bay windows, I watched snow fall lightly. Padre and I were on the sofa. Silver was in the papasan chair Lisa had gotten at her favorite store, Pier I Imports.

She came into the room dressed for work, which was dressed for TV: the conservative white blouse to go with the black skirt. Over the blouse, she also had on a blazer, which matched the skirt. I had never known the ins and outs of women's hair and how they did it, but Lisa's was magnificent—the color of wet tar, shoulder-length, and wavy. The same went for her makeup—I could tell she had it on because I knew the before and after versions; but, aside from lipstick, I couldn't see where it had been applied.

"Wow, girl," Silver said.

We stood and Lisa and Silver exchanged kisses on the cheek.

"If you're jealous," Silver said, "I can kiss you, too." He started toward me.

I held up my hand. "No thanks."

They giggled. She shook Padre's hand. "Brian."

"How are you?"

"Tired." She grinned and pointed at me. "Trying to take care of this one."

"You're off to work, so you got me two babysitters?" I said.

Lisa and Silver stared at each other. "No, sweetie. Tim's helping me."

"The tie," I said. "Of course. What're you working on?"

He glanced at Lisa.

"Uh-huh," I said. "Lisa, what's going on?"

"Jack, you keep your secret. I'll keep mine."

"Wonderful," I said.

"I told you," she said. "I'm all over this story."

I had figured as much.

"I know Hutch Gainer came to our suite the night before your assault," she said.

If *HOLY SHIT* were a facial expression, I'd have been wearing it. My recovery was weak: "A lot of Tour buddies visit me on the road, Lisa. Padre came here to see me."

"Not at 3:00 A.M. Anyway, you won't help me help you, so I called Tim."

Silver was looking at the floor.

Padre broke the silence: "Help you with what, Lisa?"

No one responded.

"Lisa," I said, "look how well things are going here. Let it go."

"It's my job, Jack, my career."

"Guys," I said, "can we have a minute?"

"Sure," Padre said. "We'll take a ride."

\* \* \*

"It's going well, huh?" She crossed her arms and tilted her head. We were standing in the kitchen. The door had just closed behind Silver and Padre.

"I mean, I'm happy," I said.

"Well, I'm not," she said. "Not that it matters."

"It does matter."

"Apparently not."

I sighed and went to the kitchen table. Sunlight drifted through sliding glass doors that led to a back deck.

"Lisa," I said, "I've never been in a situation like this. I'm caught between my heart and the rest of me."

"What?"

"If I don't do this," I said, "I couldn't be who I am. And you love me because of who I am."

"It's for the game, isn't it?"

I nodded.

"I have a career, too," she said. "And part of what makes me who I am is my career, Jack."

"I know."

"So we're stuck."

"I think so."

"I'm going to find out what Hutch Gainer was doing in our suite at three o'clock in the morning."

# Chapter Eleven

—

THEY HAD ARRIVED in a large Suburban. I had never seen any of them before. My conversation with Lisa had ended only minutes earlier. She had started brewing a fresh pot of coffee and had set a travel mug on the counter. When the foursome came to the front door, she turned from the counter and looked at the men, then at me, and I knew she wasn't leaving.

All four wore suits, but none looked like businessmen. The man in back had a lined, weathered face and appeared 60. The one in front was probably in his 40s and wore two nickel-sized rings. Next to him was a young guy who had the neck and emitted the standard attitude problem of a bodybuilder. The third guy was short and thin and wore wire-rimmed glasses.

If you walked into a restaurant and saw this group sitting there, you'd sit across the room.

"Don't open the door." I went upstairs to the master bedroom, opened a bureau drawer, and retrieved Perkins's .22 automatic. The flat four-inch barrel was cold on my skin. It held 11 rounds and Perkins had given me plenty of ammo. I loaded the gun. With it in the waistband of my jeans, I pulled my T-shirt out so it hung over and went back downstairs.

Lisa was standing, hands on hips, waiting.

"I'll get the door," I said.

"You know these people?" she said.

"No. But I don't want you answering—"

"I answer the door in my home." She pulled it open. "Can I

help you?"

The one in front said: "We'd like to speak with Mr. Austin."

"He's convalescing," she said. "Maybe in several weeks."

"We've come a long way, Ms. Trembley," the guy in the glasses said.

"How do you know my name? Who are you?"

We were all quiet. The refrigerator hummed softly.

"My name is Frank Rosselli," the one in front wearing rings said. "May we come inside?"

I moved behind Lisa. The close-up showed Rosselli to be compact without being fat, with a full pate of graying black hair. He wore a red tie with blue and gray golfers.

"What do you want with Jack?" Lisa said.

I thought it a good question.

"We're golf fans who've come from East Texas to see how he is feeling. This older gentleman is Mr. Pasqual Smittinoni. This strapping fellow is Rocky Moore. And finally, the small gentleman with glasses is Thomas Gianni."

"You came all the way from Texas to check on Jack's health?"

The air seemed tension-filled and thick. Yet I wanted them to come in; maybe I could find something out.

But Lisa was here. "Honey, why don't you go to work. I'll talk with these gentlemen."

She shook her head. I was a simple annoyance, like a fly to someone trying to read. Her focus remained on them.

"Do you know anything about the assault?" she said.

"I see," Frank said. "No. Sorry, but we know nothing of that. We were in Houston when it happened." He looked past her to me. "I'm sorry, Jack. Can I call you Jack?"

I didn't say anything.

"A real shame," Frank went on. "Your putting was starting to come around."

"Must be a big fan," I said.

"I am. Rock, get the gift."

We stood in silence as the weightlifter went to the truck and returned with a jewelry box. Rosselli took it and handed it to Lisa. "For you, Jack. Please open it."

I moved within two feet of Rosselli. "Lisa, get back."

"I'm insulted," he said.

"And I'm careful."

When she had moved, I opened it. Inside was a money clip.

"Gold," Frank said.

"I can't accept this."

Rosselli held up a hand and shook his head. "A get-well present."

Everyone was quiet. In my palm, the money clip was heavy. Real gold.

"Lisa," I said, "why don't you go to the TV station?"

"Have we interrupted something?" Frank said. "We should've called ahead."

Lisa stared at me, trying to get an idea as to my thoughts. I wanted her out of the house. I didn't know who they were, but if they had come for a hit they could've done it when I had walked, earlier that morning. Which made me feel stupid for having not taken the gun with me. If I let them in, I might learn something about what was going on with Hutch Gainer.

Lisa's stare was now laser-like. "I'm staying," she said.

\* \* \*

I held the door and we went to the living room. Lisa and I sat on the love seat. The .22 dug into me, but the T-shirt hung loosely and kept it out of sight. Gianni sat next to Rosselli on the sofa. The old man was in a rocking chair near the unlit fireplace and moved back and forth slowly. Rocky, looking petulant, stood near Rosselli. There was a small bulge near his left armpit. It didn't take a genius to know what it was.

"I don't know why you're here," I said, "but I assume it's not to shoot me, so please put the guns on the coffee table where I can see them."

No one moved. They all seemed to glance covertly at Rosselli. Except nothing is covert when three people do it at once.

Frank said: "Do it."

The one with glasses, Gianni, made a face, but removed a gun that looked much like Perkins's 9 mm automatic pistol. It was the color of an old bruise and very flat. He laid it gently on the coffee table. "Want me to use a coaster?" he said.

"Tommy," the old man, Smittinoni, stopped rocking. "Don't go uninvited into someone's home then wisecrack. Shut your mouth."

Frank looked over his shoulder at Rocky and gave a tiny nod. The weight lifter opened his sports coat. He wore a shoulder holster and pulled the same gun as the other two. He set it on the table.

"You're an observant man," Gianni said. He had his legs crossed and his arm on the back of the sofa. He dangled his ankle effeminately.

When you spend a good deal of time with Perkins, you see most types of guns and various holsters. But they didn't need to know that.

"Beautiful home, Ms. Trembley," Frank said.

Lisa thanked him.

I said: "What did you come from Texas for?"

"We came bearing gifts."

"And I thank you," I said. "I'm leery right now. There must be more to this visit."

"We want you to play golf with us." Rosselli uncrossed his legs, leaned forward and clasped his hands in his lap.

"You came from Texas to ask me to play golf with you?"

"Yes."

Lisa was staring at Rosselli. Gianni was looking out the window; Smittinoni was rocking gently, looking absently at the floor. Rocky was admiring Lisa.

"We know," Frank said, "you're not ready to play yet, but when you're back on Tour, we'd like you to take a morning and play."

"To be honest," I said, "if I'm not playing on Tour, I'm relaxing. And when I'm on Tour all I do is play and practice. I don't have a lot of free time."

"We realize it's your livelihood," Gianni said, turning back from the window. He had a five o'clock shadow and penetrating blue eyes. "We fully expect to compensate you."

I knew corporate sponsors paid guys like Greg Norman and Chi Chi Rodriguez a hundred grand a day to play the first hole of an event with each threesome, walking the first hole, riding a cart back to the tee, and playing the hole again—over and over, chatting, and basically being a celebrity. But those guys were celebrities. I was still trying to win my first event.

"Corporate outing?" I said.

"More or less."

"What's more or less a corporate outing?" Lisa said.

All eyes went to Rosselli. He cleared his throat. "My company is Frank Rosselli Industries."

"Out of?" Lisa said.

"Houston."

"Where's the event?" I said.

"Still undecided," Gianni said. "Look, we come here, give you a money clip worth two grand, then offer you a good deal—$10,000, maybe more, for a morning—and you treat us like criminals. Frankly, we don't need this."

"Why not just call?" I said.

"Mr. Rosselli likes to do business in person," Gianni said. He liked talking. There was no doubt he worked for Rosselli—they all did—but I could tell he liked being in charge.

"Tommy thought it would be better to go and personally invite you," Frank said. "Maybe that was a mistake."

Gianni shook his head vehemently.

"Tell us more about the golf event," Lisa said. "It's for the people in your company?"

"Just a fun competition."

"A tournament?" I said.

"Rocky, please warm up the car," Frank said. Rocky went out. "We've taken too much of your time. We'll go now, but we'd like to count you in."

There was only one way to find out what these guys were up to. "Sure," I said. Then I felt Lisa's eyes on the side of my face again.

# Chapter Twelve

———

ON A MONDAY EVENING, less than three weeks after I'd been assaulted, we were in Albuquerque for the Holiday Inn Southwest Open. Golf was on the rise in the Southwest and the Tour was capitalizing on that, having an event there. I was back, and Lisa was making a bigger deal of it than I wanted—champagne and shrimp, balloons and streamers. And a banner that read WELCOME BACK, JACK!!! strewn across the ceiling in the hotel conference room. She had invited every player in the field, his wife or girl-friend, and caddie. Silver was not present; he was holed up in a motel in New York working on his book. I had introduced Perkins as my new caddie. Several players glanced at him from across the room. At six-five, with an offensive lineman's build, he stood out among golfers.

Across the room, Lisa was talking to Padre and two other players. I had the pleasure of being stuck between Tom Schilling, who was in golf attire, and detective Mike Chee, who wore shorts and dark socks. Perkins was next to me, sipping a beer. I had declined one, but when Schilling said a hotel-records check of Tucson for the week of my assault turned up four of Houston's finest, I thought of Rosselli and felt I needed a drink. When he said none of the thugs could be located, I was ready for a double.

Schilling was drinking Diet Coke from a glass and chewing the ice. He said: "All these guys have priors and are on the greaseball checklist anytime something goes down in Houston."

"Take a look at this." Chee waved a manila folder at me.

It contained rap sheets and photos. All four faces were unshaven, fleshy, with the flat fish-eyed stare people give in mug shots. I thought back to the chase; all had worn sunglasses. I couldn't place any of these faces.

"Senior class at MIT?" I said.

Perkins chuckled.

"Funny," Chee said. "Recognize any?"

"Sorry," I said.

Schilling's ice grinding could be heard above the room's steady banter.

"They had sunglasses on," I said.

"Jack," Chee said, "the chances of these four coming to Tucson the same weekend you were assaulted is far too big a coincidence."

"Maybe they're golf fans."

"Un uh."

"Might have come to look at snakes," I said.

Chee ignored that one. "Anyone say anything that you recall?"

"No."

"You want my theory," Schilling said. He didn't wait for me to decline. "They were bumped after the job." He went on chewing his ice.

"On that note," Chee said, "what do you know about John Pickorino?" He glanced at me and did not blink.

It had my full attention.

"He visited you in the hospital," Chee said.

"Bunch of people did," I said. "I don't know him. Said he was a big golf fan, seemed like a nice old man."

"Either of you know his, ah, occupation?" Schilling said.

Perkins was looking around the room, appearing totally uninterested.

I wondered how I was doing. I liked Chee. He was doing a difficult job and working hard at it—for my sake; Schilling, however, was probably trying to make a name for himself.

"He's been in organized crime since conception," Chee said. "Done a total of nine months in County for attempted murder. Been known to have personally clipped 20 or more adversaries. Loan sharking, dealing, probably a pimp, too. If it goes down in New Orleans, he's got a hand in it."

I thought of the blue car at Lisa's. Someone had been keeping tabs on me. Could have been Pickorino. Or maybe Rosselli and gang. Hell, it might've been Schilling; he knew I was withholding info.

"Jack," Chee said, "guys like Pickorino don't play games."

"Sounds like it," I said, trying to sound surprised.

"That mean we've still heard all you've got?" Schilling said. "Hard to believe no one said a thing to you in that alley. They just assaulted you? No one spoke?"

"Wrong place at the wrong time. I'm trying to move on. A lot of people here to welcome me back. I should mingle."

I took two steps and saw Hutch Gainer walk in.

In cowboy boots, a jean shirt, skintight blue jeans, and a Stetson hat, he stood out among the polo-shirt-and-khakis crowd as definitely as Perkins. Behind him was the gallery: Kiko, the tough Latino Perkins had dropped; the blonde, Jenna; and the man of the hour, John Pickorino.

Pickorino wasted no time. With Kiko behind him, he left Jenna and Hutch and walked over casually and shook my hand. Kiko glared at Perkins, who smiled at him.

Schilling nearly choked on his ice; Chee played it cool.

Pickorino said: "Officers."

"We're not cops," Schilling said.

It made Pickorino smile. He said to me: "You look fit, better than ever."

"I don't know," Perkins said, "can't shine shit."

The smile widened.

"It's been almost a month," I said.

"How's your game?" Pickorino said.

"I shot par this morning. I don't really know. As soon as I could hit balls painfree, I got the O.K. from my doctor, and here I am."

Schilling still hadn't recovered; Chee was listening to every word.

"Kiko, perhaps you could get me something to drink."

"Johnny," Kiko said, "I'd better stay. Jenna'll get it."

"Kiko, I told you to get it. If you won't," Pickorino winked at Perkins, "I'll have this large man knock you around again."

Chee's eyes ran to mine and he raised his brows.

Pickorino's head swiveled slowly. "*Now*, Kiko."

Kiko went for the drink.

"Officers," Pickorino said, "may I speak with Jack in private?"

Schilling muttered something and Chee said, "Sure." They walked to the other side of the room.

When he was certain they were out of earshot, Pickorino said: "I may be close to getting some information, but something strange is going on. When I get details, I will let you know."

"What do you mean by strange?"

"I don't know, but now maybe you can help me," Pickorino said. "Hutch is in an awful slump. I don't know what to do. And he's in pain—a stomach virus or something that won't quit."

I looked across the room and saw Hutch, sitting by himself, pale and tired, looking out the window. He was young and seemed very alone.

"Slumps can be tough," I said.

"It seems more than that," Pickorino said, watching him. "He doesn't practice, and he's losing weight and won't eat."

Perkins was biting his lip in deep thought.

I told Pickorino I'd talk to Hutch. We shook hands again and he left. Hutch never made eye contact on the way out. I stood, thinking about Pickorino's "strange" comment, until Schilling and Chee came back.

\* \* \*

"What would a scumbag like that be doing around the Tour?" Schilling said.

"Golf fan," Perkins said.

"You don't buy that any more than we do," Chee said. "You worked homicide for the PD in Boston. Got yourself in a jam, so you quit."

"Been doing your homework," Perkins said.

"It's my job."

"Heard you beat the hell out of a guy who deserved it. A child molester."

Perkins stared at him, sipped his beer, and said: "I don't think why I quit is your business."

As if on cue, Lisa, in a caramel-colored top and matching sundress, appeared. Schilling was engrossed in her every move. I didn't much like that.

"What happened between you and the Mexican?" Schilling said to Perkins.

"The accent says he's from Puerto Rico," Chee said.

"Same difference," Schilling said. "You two get into it?"

"Think I'll get another beer," Perkins said and left.

Lisa kissed my cheek. "Nice to see all your friends, isn't it?"

"Thanks for the party," I said.

"Mr. Rosselli is a very nice man," she said. "When I explained I'm working on a feature about Texas companies, he offered to have me visit his, ah, 'corporate offices' in Houston."

I glared at her. She smiled like a cheerleader, batted her long lashes and walked away. I was silent, watching her go.

Perkins returned and handed me a Heineken. I took a long pull.

"You've got to be shitting me," Chee said. "Pickorino and Rosselli? What the hell are you involved in?"

That was a question I wanted answered. "Nothing," I said. "Why?"

"Why? Rosselli is what Pickorino was when Pickorino was in his prime."

Schilling said: "Crazy bastard walked into a restaurant in Mexico City when he was 19 and took out 12 people."

"Let us help you," Chee said.

"I think we've tried to help you," Schilling said. "Even your fiancée has—and judging from what she just said—still is. You're going to wind up dead."

"That's enough," Perkins said.

"You can't protect him from guys like Pickorino and Rosselli." He looked hard at Perkins. "Even if he did beat up Pickorino's thug." Schilling turned and walked out.

Chee pulled out his wallet, handed me a business card, then followed.

After a couple of moments of silence, Perkins said: "You're sweating."

"Yeah."

We drank from our beers.

"When did Rosselli come onto the scene?" he said.

I told him. We finished those beers and got two more. And he told me Vegas had provided very little information and I explained my cyber findings regarding golf and gambling.

"I'd like to know more about side bets," I said. "The stuff Hutch was blackmailed for—shooting a certain score, bogeying a hole?"

"Getting inside," he said. "That's always the difficult part."

# Chapter Thirteen

―――

TUESDAY MORNING I WOKE BEFORE DAWN, kissed Lisa without waking her, showered, and headed to the lobby for coffee and the paper before meeting Perkins. As the elevator descended, I had an uneasy sensation in the pit of my stomach.

We had a golf date with Frank Rosselli.

The restaurant was busy. The smell of bacon and coffee mixed with something that smelled of fried peppers. The clientele was split—one group ran to businesspersons in suits or skirts, toting briefcases, and sitting alone or in groups; the others were golfers, reading sports pages and stock sections, sipping coffee and juice, and eating big meals of cereal, toast, and eggs.

One man fit neither group. Sitting in a booth, looking down at the menu, wearing a black silk shirt, black jeans, and black cowboy boots, his long hair back in a ponytail, Kiko was eating alone.

Being an outgoing guy, I joined him.

He looked up but didn't speak.

"Que pasa, amigo?" I said, sliding in across from him. Outside, the parking lot was bright, thanks to streetlights. It wasn't quite six A.M.

He glanced around the room, then peered over his shoulder.

"Perkins isn't here, Kiko. What are we having?"

"What do you want?"

"Maybe French toast. Shoot the breeze. Nice of your boss to investigate my—" I searched for the word.

"Ass-kicking?"

"That will do," I said. "I'd have chosen something a little more poetic, but that works. Nice of him to investigate it for me. He come up with anything?"

"Why don't you ask him?"

"I will. Just figured you'd know. When he threw Jenna out of the hospital room, he told Hutch to stay. Said family could stay. Must consider you that as well because you were there."

Kiko drank coffee and looked bored. "Whatever, Austin."

"How long have you been with him?"

"Why do you ask?"

"No reason."

He lowered the coffee slowly. "Six years."

"Long time."

"Some days it's an eternity."

"Like last night, at the party?"

"The line about having your buddy drop me if I didn't get the drink? Yeah, that gets old."

"Where're you from?"

"What the hell is this?"

"Just curious." My father used to say smart people didn't have all the answers; they just knew where to find them. And Kiko was a starting point.

He leaned back, folded his arms across his chest, and watched me. I was quiet.

Finally, a grin broke across his face. He appeared genuinely amused. "Miami. Parents came from Puerto Rico when I was a kid, then they went back. Left me when I was 13."

"Rough," I said.

He shrugged it off.

A waitress topped Kiko's coffee. I ordered regular coffee, French toast—six pieces—with butter and syrup.

"How'd you end up in Orleans?"

"Going to school there," he said. "Saw an ad for a chauffeur. Called the number."

"Pickorino?"

"Yeah."

"Job entails a little more than driving."

He shifted in his seat. "You don't know what my job entails."

"O.K.," I said.

The waitress returned with my coffee and left. I motioned to the cream and sugar.

Kiko slid them to me. "What do you want my life story for?"

"Room's full of people with the same rap—the nine-to-five business crowd, and golfers whose story I know. Figured the conversation would be better here. What were you studying while you were in school?"

"Culinary Arts."

It was my turn to lean back and stare. "Really?"

"Saying I don't look like a chef?" He grinned and sipped his coffee.

"What's your specialty?"

"Caribbean cuisine. I got some family recipes."

"Quite a change—college life to working for Pickorino."

"College life." He shook his head. "It was night school and I wasn't a Boy Scout in Miami. Had a few run-ins, so I wanted to try New Orleans."

And there, I thought, he'd gotten mixed up with Pickorino and a crime family. No step up. "Do any cooking now?"

"For myself."

"Not for Pickorino?"

"He wouldn't appreciate it. I cook for my girlfriend."

"Girlfriend from Orleans?"

"Cut the bullshit."

I sipped my coffee.

"I'm not going to be with Pickorino forever." He glanced out the window. "Pay's good. Saving money to buy a joint—a diner or a little restaurant."

"And you'll cook?"

"I'll do it all—cook, scrub dishes, run the register."

Outside, the sun was peeking over the Sandia Mountains.

"How'd you go from driver to what you're doing now?"

"And what's that?"

"Hitting for Pickorino."

"You know for a fact that I'm a shooter?"

"No."

"It's a fucking insult being called that."

The waitress returned with my meal.

We were silent a while as I ate. Then he said: "You got nerve calling me that. Look at your life—money, travel, the broad."

His response had been genuine and I felt the full weight of it. I set my fork down. "I've got it good. I know that. I didn't mean to insult you. I apologize."

"Fuck you."

At the far end of the restaurant, above the bar, the TV played the morning news. Outside, people were walking to cars with paper coffee cups and folded newspapers.

He got up and tossed $2 on the table.

"Kiko," I said.

He looked at me.

"If you don't shoot people, why don't you describe your duties to me?"

He stared at me a long time. Then he turned and walked out.

I finished my meal, had one more cup of coffee, and sat looking out the window at Frank Rosselli, Tommy Gianni, and Rocky waiting in the parking lot, sipping coffee and chatting around a stretch limo. The sky above them was vast and full of promise. I was almost optimistic.

* * *

In the lobby, I met Perkins, who was at the courtesy breakfast counter pouring coffee into a large white Styrofoam cup.

"They're waiting for us," I said.

He smiled.

We had set things up to appear authentic—he came down with my clubs, as if, so dedicated, he hadn't wanted them out of his sight, or—should anyone ask—I had told him to say he had taken them to his room to regrip last night. Frank wouldn't know the Tour had an equipment trailer.

In the bag, he had a 9 mm. I had something more important next to it.

"What'll you say if they search the bag?" he said.

"You're paranoid and have a gun permit."

"I meant the other thing. You better have a good excuse."

"I know."

"And you have a good excuse?"

"You seen those Hertz commercials?"

"'Not exactly?'" he said. "Great. We'll end up part of some building's foundation in Houston."

"I don't see them searching every inch of that bag. That would make this outing seem a little suspicious, wouldn't it?"

"Guys like this don't take chances, Jack."

Outside, Frank waved. I returned the gesture. The parking lot was busy. I was dressed for golf—khakis, navy blue sleeveless sweater over a striped shirt, and soft-spiked shoes. Perkins wore blue jean shorts, a white T-shirt, running shoes, a Titleist hat I'd given him, and dark aviator shades.

When we reached them, the sight wasn't pretty: Frank looked like he'd raided Fred Couples' closet—blue and white striped Ashworth shirt, navy blue pants, and a white visor. He shifted when he saw us and I heard his spikes tap and click on the pavement. Clothes or not, he didn't look like an athlete. However, Tommy Gianni was worse; he wore knickers—and long white socks, a Kangol hat, and $300 gold-tipped golf shoes. Rocky was in uniform: a sports jacket over T-shirt, and jeans.

Frank shook my hand. "Looking good, Jack. Ride with us."

"I've got a courtesy car."

"You both can ride with us."

"Sure," I said.

Rocky took the clubs from Perkins and put them in the trunk. Perkins and I climbed in the limo and sat next to Gianni, across from Rosselli and Rocky.

"You going to fit inside here?" Frank said to Perkins.

"Might be tight," Perkins said.

"How far is the ride?" I said.

"Forty-five minutes," Tommy said. "You in a hurry?"

I didn't say anything.

"Small Boy," Frank said.

Gianni turned to him.

"Give Jack his money."

I liked the nickname for Gianni. He *was* small. Not only in stature, but also in the fact that he was clearly a number-two man, yet striving to carry himself like Frank's equal. Tommy motioned to Rocky, who opened his sports jacket and retrieved an envelope from his pocket. The motion confirmed what I had assumed; both Perkins and I saw the revolver in Rocky's shoulder holster.

The envelope contained cash—hundred-dollar bills. I did not count it. "Not many appearance fees are paid in cash."

"Well, I'm running this operation," Tommy said. "And this ain't the Tour. You don't like it, I can find good use for ten grand in bills."

"Tommy," Frank said, "know what Pasqual Smittinoni would say?"

Gianni didn't answer.

"He'd say shut your mouth. You want more responsibility, earn it."

"The elderly man?" I said.

"Yes," Frank said, "a father to me. He's home this week."

Perkins was quiet, watching and listening.

Tommy sat staring at Frank.

Rosselli caught Gianni's gaze and reached over and slapped his face hard, leaving a red blotch. In the contained area, the sound was like the crack of a bat. The two men sat looking hard at each other for several long moments. Then Tommy turned away.

"I'm not going to be embarrassed by incompetence, Tommy," Frank said. "I take care of you and always have."

The sound of men breathing in and out was the only sound for what seemed a long time.

"I hope my guests can excuse this," Frank said.

Neither Perkins nor I spoke.

"Now tell them about the match, Tommy."

Gianni pulled himself together quickly. As he had at Lisa's home, he quickly shifted into leadership gear. Leaning back, putting one arm along the back of the seat, he smiled.

"It's like this," he said. "Lowest combined score wins the hole. Fifteen grand for the front, fifteen for the back, and a side bet: fifteen grand for the eighteen-hole total score, counting handicaps of the amateurs."

"We're a foursome?"

"You and I," Frank said, "are a twosome."

"Against whom?"

"You got questions," Tommy said, "direct them to me. This is my deal. You're our guy. They bring the best they can find. Two pros, two"—he motioned to Rosselli—"amateurs."

"My high handicap will help us for the total score," Frank said. "We'll split all earnings. But the money isn't important to me."

"Who are we playing against?"

Tommy glanced at Frank, then said: "A...business associate."

# Chapter Fourteen

———

AT LEAST THE WEATHER was perfect: high-sixties and sunny. That was what I was thinking as we walked from the range to the first tee. My ribs had felt only slightly sore warming up and I was hitting the ball well. But my mind wasn't on golf; if I was to gain any insight into what was going on, I had to play. And I felt like a prostitute. *Ten grand's all you need. For a good golf time, call Jack.* At least I was high-priced.

Rocky was caddying for Frank, who stood across the first tee from Perkins and me, mentally preparing—eyes closed, breathing in and out slowly.

Perkins set my bag down and crossed his huge arms. I took the envelope out of my back pocket and handed it to him. "Start a college fund for Jackie."

"I wondered how an Eagle Scout like you would handle that."

"I don't need the money," I said. "Take it."

"You don't have so much that ten grand doesn't mean anything. You can't take it because it's dirty."

"Just take it."

"Thanks." He put the envelope in the golf bag.

Gianni approached, carrying a muffin. "We're having a party afterwards."

Perkins seemed relaxed; my stomach was churning.

Gianni had transformed into the confident leader again. I figured it had a lot to do with Frank being out of earshot.

"Jack," Tommy said, "standard procedure is I pat you down

———

and look through your bag."

Perkins stood peering behind dark aviator shades; the tip of his tongue ran along his upper lip.

"No problem with that?" Tommy asked.

"It's your event. You said 'standard procedure.' You have these matches often?"

"Occasionally."

"This is interesting," I said. "Never had my bag searched at a golf tournament before."

"Big business. In business, you can't trust people."

Still holding the muffin, he ran a hand up and down my sides, up the front of my legs, and felt outside my khaki pockets. As he did, my body made several reflex movements. He went to Perkins, who stood stoically throughout the procedure.

Then Gianni reached for the bag with his free hand. One hand or not, he would not miss the gun or my tape recorder.

"Tommy," I said.

He froze. "Yeah?"

"Had problems at these things before?"

"What?" My clubs clacked against each other as he moved them side to side. "What do you consider a problem?"

I saw a partial opening and ran for it. "Just figured you wouldn't be searching me if I had your trust. Kind of insulting."

He stopped and looked up. "You insulted?"

"Yeah."

"No offense. Just business."

He unzipped a side pocket.

I quickly knelt beside him. "Hey—a company sends me a year's supply of tees. You're a golfer. Here, take some." I pulled out a fistful.

"Got no place to put these," he said. He still had his muffin.

"Put them in your bag. They're extra strength, professional quality." I was speaking gibberish now, but Gianni was listening.

I unzipped a second pocket. "Got some balls in here." I handed him two sleeves.

He held them on top of the tees, a muffin in one hand, free goodies in the other.

The only pocket left was the one he couldn't go through—with the gun and my hand-held, voice-activated recorder.

I partially unzipped it, rummaged, and pulled out a Titleist towel and handed it to him. "You can buy the other things, but only the pros get these. Here." I held it out. Gianni's hands were both full.

"Thanks, Jack," he said. "Hey, Rock, come here."

Gianni handed the muffin, tees, and balls to Rocky. He unfolded the towel and examined it. "Thanks." He took the stuff back from Rocky, who left again to stand near Frank.

"I'm playing with a group of businessmen behind you guys." Gianni winked. "Big deals I've got to close."

"What's it like working in big business?" I said.

"Got to know what you're doing."

Apparently, the search was now complete.

"Got to know how to wheel and deal. That's how you get to the top."

"To get this club to yourselves for a day, you must be at the top."

"Yeah, Franky's done O.K. I always knew he would."

"Been together a long time?" I said it as if they were equals.

"Since first grade."

Rosselli's comment in the car—*I've always taken care of you*—made sense.

"How do you feel, Jack?" Frank said, approaching. "You ready?" He glanced at Gianni.

"Sure," I said.

"The slugs we're playing are inside eating. I'll go tell them we're ready."

He went into the clubhouse. Gianni moved to the other side of the tee and looked down the fairway. He lit a cigarette and seemed in deep thought. I suspected the wheeling and dealing wasn't as easy as he made it out to be.

I reached into the bag and clicked on the recorder. When I rezipped the pocket, I left it partially open.

Perkins was watching. "I got a bad feeling about that goddamned recorder. How long's that thing run?"

"Three hours."

"Won't be long enough."

"It's voice-activated. If we cut the chitchat, it'll only pick up what we want."

"And what's that?"

"Whatever we can get."

"Won't we be too far away?" Perkins said.

"That's where I come in."

He rolled his eyes.

* * *

Frank led two men and their caddies onto the first tee. One was obviously the Rosselli of the twosome, except prettier—long blond hair and dressed head to toe in Tommy Hilfiger. Next to him was the ace: a short guy with something on his lip that might or might not have constituted a moustache. I'd never seen him before.

"I really want this match, Jack," Frank whispered.

"Who are they?"

"Come meet them."

I followed him and the blonde guy extended his hand.

"Jack," Frank said, "this is Ronnie Giacomin."

"Jack Austin," I said.

"Yeah. I know who you are. Meet Tom Phillips. He's a Buy.com Tour player who's going to give you a lesson today."

"Think so?" I shook hands with Phillips.

"Never had a Tour player come out," Giacomin said. "You need the money?"

"Makes the world go around," I said.

"Can't be a legitimate Tour player if you need the money."

"I've been out there 10 years."

"We here for a bar fight or to play golf?" Perkins said.

"Yeah," Frank said. "Let's get going."

Rosselli and Giacomin reviewed their handicaps. I took out my three-wood and loosened up, swinging it back and forth slowly.

I was there to get Frank to tell me something about gambling on the PGA Tour, a statement to confirm that it was happening. And, of course, I needed names. Given Hutch's situation and the fact that Rosselli had driven nearly an hour so he could gamble, the odds—no pun intended—were pretty good he would have information.

As Phillips and I walked back to the gold tees—about 50 yards behind the whites—I had a strange sensation of being totally and completely alone. A golf course seemed strange without people. And to a guy used to playing before thousands, the feeling was odd. I wondered when the rest of the so-called corporation was going to show.

* * *

The first hole was a par five, 505 yards from the whites, 560 from the gold tees. The fairway didn't look very wide.

"A three-wood, huh? I heard you were long," Phillips said.

"For control. How much you getting for this?"

"Five grand and half the winnings. You?"

I don't know if I lied out of modesty or if I was ashamed to be a higher-priced golf prostitute than he was, but I simply said: "Same."

"I need that money for Qualifying School."

"That's why you're here?" I made a good pass at the ball and held a well-balanced follow-through.

"Yeah. Easy money. Five Gs to show up? Come on."

"You know Giacomin well?"

"Not really."

Phillips hit a drive into the heart of the fairway but short of my ball.

As we walked to the white tees, I thought about the costs of trying to break into the PGA Tour. Phillips was falling into the same trap as Hutch Gainer.

For a moment, I found myself feeling sorry for the kid. But, as he'd said, it was "easy money." I thought back to my Tour beginnings. Easy money? I'd spent my whole first season sleeping in the back of a rusted-out station wagon.

\* \* \*

I had 260 yards to the pear-shaped first green. After the others hit layup shots, I took the three-wood again. I had never played the course before, but the map on the scorecard showed the green was guarded by two large bunkers. Rosselli, Giacomin, Phillips, and their caddies were walking up the fairway toward Perkins and me.

"Can you reach that?" Perkins said.

"For a guy who claims to never watch the sport on TV you know my game pretty well."

"Seen you hit a lot of bad shots."

"Cute," I said. "I don't care if Rosselli wins. I'm going for every flag today and testing my side."

I put the ball in a front bunker. Perkins only chuckled.

Finally, we walked over to Rosselli. Phillips and Giacomin were talking strategy on the other side of the fairway. I gave Perkins a look and he—and the recorder—moved closer.

"You've got a really solid swing, Frank," I said. "What's your handicap?"

He looked across the fairway at Giacomin, then winked at me. "A 19."

Great. He was a sandbagger, too.

"You've got a natural draw and a really well-balanced swing.

You could be scratch."

"Certainly. Just need to play more."

"That's the key," I said. "How many Tour events you go to each year?"

"As many as I can."

"You don't mind walking or the heat? Wouldn't it be easier to watch some on TV?"

"I like to be in the action."

"That's why I like playing for money," I said. "During practice rounds I usually put some money down."

Rosselli took a practice swing. "Like boxing," he said. "Everyone for themselves. You see who can stand up to the pressure, who can survive."

\* \* \*

At the green, I climbed into the bunker with my 60-degree wedge. The pin was in the center, so I had plenty of green to work with and could let the ball release to the hole instead of trying to stop it or spin it back. If I executed, the shot wouldn't be difficult.

I opened my front foot and actually aimed 10 yards left. Then I tried to slide the open face of the wedge under the ball and cut across it, pushing it on line. I put the ball within three feet.

Frank said to Giacomin: "Jack's first on. We're up a grand."

Giacomin and Rosselli had both missed the green with their respective third shots; Phillips had left his 30 yards from the hole, which surprised me—the Buy.com Tour is top-notch—and made me wonder how he was faring. He putted first and did well, leaving himself a tap-in par. Rosselli made bogey; Giacomin made double. My three-foot birdie putt was to win the hole.

Rosselli must've read the putt five times.

I dropped the birdie into the heart of the cup. Rosselli high-fived me again.

"First on and first in," he said. "Two grand and we win the first hole."

If this kept up, he'd offer me a job.

He smiled at Giacomin. "Good business is surrounding yourself with winners, Ronnie."

\* \* \*

We won the front nine, three and one. We were up four

strokes as well. And Rosselli was making more money on side bets: greenies, sandies, first-ons, and the like. Walking off the ninth green, I said: "Can I ask you something, Frank?"

Perkins moved into position.

"Sure, Jack." He slapped my back. Winning had made us golf buddies.

"I'm in some money trouble. I need to make some quick cash. This is great and easy, but I need big money very soon and I'm not into loans."

"You talking about getting in on a business deal?" Frank asked. "I don't do that. Business is business, pleasure is pleasure. This is pleasure."

He was serious now. He was also smart.

"I'm no businessman. That's your world, and judging from what I see, you're very successful."

"I am."

I didn't have time to explain the benefits of modesty to him and I wasn't sure I knew them myself. "I'm talking about giving you my money and hoping you can double or triple it—gambling. Like you said, you know how to surround yourself with winners."

As he considered that, his smile told me he liked it. "I got a guy in Vegas I deal with, but if 10 grand is a lot to you, this guy is out of your price range."

"I hear there's some gambling going on around the Tour."

He shifted and stared at me. "Really?" There was something in his eyes that Perkins had occasionally flashed at people—a look that said he would kill you without a second thought.

The muscles at the back of my neck got tight. "Yeah," I said.

Rosselli moved closer to me, arms folded. "Jack, that almost sounded like you were asking me if there is anything going on around the Tour."

This wasn't like dealing with Gianni. "I know you bet. That's why we're here. And I know you win, because you can afford this place. I'd like to give you some money to put down. That's all. If it's on Tour, I can follow it. In Vegas, I wouldn't know what my money was doing."

The glare in his eyes lightened. "I'm not Charles fucking Schwab. You're a nice guy, Jack, maybe even a friend, but I got to be honest. Don't get involved in stuff you know nothing about. People get in trouble doing that."

And with that, I grabbed my three-wood and walked back to the gold tees.

# Chapter Fifteen

———

ROSSELLI WALKED AROUND the inside of the spectacular clubhouse as if we'd won the Ryder Cup. We had closed out the back nine by winning holes 10 through 14. Neither Giacomin nor Phillips stayed for the "business outing."

The interior of the dining room was not Southwest, but rather like something from Long Island: hardwood floors, fireplaces on three walls, bookshelves lined with leather editions, and leather and mahogany furniture. Wall-to-wall carpeting felt three inches thick beneath my spikes. I sat at the bar next to Perkins and in the midst of a hundred of Frank Rosselli's closest friends, all of whom were dressed in golf attire, and seemed to be slurping drinks.

It gave me the urge to shower.

Perkins drank beer; I worked on a glass of orange juice.

"What?" he said. "You got a cold?"

"Beer dehydrates you."

"It dehydrates *you*," Perkins said.

"Jack," Gianni was suddenly at my side and handed me an envelope. "This is 15 thou for your match. Congratulations on the win." A stocky man, dressed immaculately in an ironed shirt and golf pants that were neatly creased, was beside him with short brown hair spiked and jelled into place.

The bartender mixed something that looked like a mudslide and ice cubes clanked as he shook the concoction. The envelope lay on the bar in front of me. Twenty-five grand for Jackie's college fund. If Perkins and I kept this up we'd put the kid through med school.

———

Perkins sat staring straight into the mirror across from us.

"Joey," Gianni said, "want a drink?"

The *GQ* cover boy nodded and sat down. Gianni straddled a stool next to me.

"Frank says you hit it so far it's not even fair," he said. "I'm sure you had to carry him. Golf's my game. Started playing in high school—when Frank was mister star basketball player. He called me a sissy for playing golf then."

I sipped some orange juice and extended my hand to the guy next to Gianni. "Jack Austin."

"I know," *GQ* said. He didn't shake.

"Telepathic?" I said.

"Cute. Tommy, I'm getting something to eat."

"Joey, the food's coming later."

"I don't wait." He walked off.

"Friendly," I said.

"They don't pay him to be friendly," Gianni said.

Perkins's eyes went to Gianni.

"Does he work for Frank?" I asked.

"Let me buy you guys another drink."

The room was very loud, giving it the feel of a fraternity party in the New York City Public Library. Also, there were no females.

"There's no women here," I said.

"This is a golf day. I think Frank's girlfriend is coming but that's it."

"He told me he was married."

"He is," Gianni said.

"I see."

"He's got this blonde, used to strip in Houston. Hot and knows what she's doing in the sack, according to Frank."

"How long have you lived in Houston?" I said.

"All my life."

"That how you met Frank?"

"Yeah." He drank from a dark shot glass.

"Whiskey?"

"Wild Turkey," he said.

I almost shivered. Wild Turkey for lunch.

"How long have you and Frank been together?"

"Too long."

I thought of Frank slapping him in the car. My orange juice was gone.

Gianni nodded to the bartender. "Another screwdriver for

my friend."

I couldn't tell a guy who drank Wild Turkey for lunch I was having orange juice.

"Anyway, Frank and I grew up on the same street. He was the toughest sonofabitch you ever saw. I got in with him in high school."

I looked around. "Looks like you guys do pretty well."

"Sure," he said. "Jack, you like blow?"

"Cocaine?"

"Yeah. Want a couple lines?"

Perkins's head turned slowly toward us.

"No thanks," I said. "Here's the man himself."

Rosselli sat on the stool next to Perkins. A blonde sat beside him. Jenna, Pickorino's girlfriend, didn't recognize me. I was glad her hand was no longer bruised.

I glanced at Perkins. He knew who she was. "Going to the bathroom," he said and leaned close to me as he stood. "You're not as unforgettable as I am."

Jenna's eyes followed him when he left.

Rosselli slid onto Perkins's vacant seat and ordered Jenna a screwdriver. That made me feel tough—I was at a mob convention, drinking whatever the girls were having.

"Jack," Frank said, "this is Jenna Andrews."

I shook her hand and tried not to make eye contact.

"Jack is my new golf partner, Sweet Thing. Should've seen us rip the hearts out of those two slugs and eat them."

"You have to be so graphic?" she said, looking at me.

"Sorry, Sugar, we trampled them. Have a drink. Maybe it'll loosen you up."

"I don't like vodka." Her eyes narrowed on me.

"If you're here," Frank said, "you're going to do what I tell you."

She ignored that. "Do I know you?" she said to me.

"You watch golf?" I said.

"I don't like to, but I have to sometimes."

Frank said: "This is Jack Austin. Ever hear of him?"

She had the looks for the job, but lacked the ability—she was no actress. "No."

"Not exactly a household name." I wondered what she had heard and from whom. Did she remember me from the hospital room?

Big Band music began to play. I turned around and saw a waitresses carrying trays of lunch platters.

"Lobster rolls," Frank said.

"In New Mexico?" I said.

"Had it flown in from Maine last night."

"Sweetie, how 'bout you run along, get me lunch?" Frank said.

"I'm not a waitress."

He pounded his open palm down on the bar.

She flinched and left.

* * *

"You know what I gave Small Boy for Christmas?" Frank said. We were eating lobster rolls.

I was going to guess a Colombian drug lord, but thought he might not see the holiday spirit in that.

"A Rolls Royce. Tommy will never be able to afford one himself. That's how I treat my friends. Where's Chrissani?"

"Went looking for something to eat," Gianni said.

"Alone?"

"He's a guest," Gianni said.

"He's your guest and I don't trust him."

Perkins came back, sat next to Gianni, and asked for a beer.

The bartender took my glass to refill it. I shook my head.

"What about your enemies?" I said. "How do you treat them?"

"My enemies?" Frank said. He looked around, then at me for a long moment. He was considering something. One of his brows raised in appraisal of the question. Then he glanced at Perkins and absently touched his chin, thinking. The four of us sat quietly for several moments, then to Gianni, he said: "Could you two excuse Jack and me for a moment?"

Perkins shrugged, got his beer, and left the bar. Gianni went as well, but with an expression that said he felt left out. I knew Rosselli was about say something important. He didn't want anyone to hear but me, keeping things—*mano y mano*—my word against his.

"Make no mistake, Jack," he said. "A guy once took 20 grand from me. So I fixed that problem." He gave a tiny hand flutter, as if the problem had been a fly and he had simply swatted it. "Went to his house one night, got him out of bed, and walked him to his backyard. His old lady and little girl were in the window when I put a .44 Magnum in his ear and blew his brains out the other side, all over the lawn."

"Jesus Christ." It was out before I could stop it. But he smiled as if pleased. My reaction had been what he'd wanted.

"Weak stomach, Jack?" he said.

I wished I'd had my recorder.

Jenna sat back down and set a second plate of lobster rolls in front of him. Rosselli called to Perkins and Gianni, "Come, eat," he said graciously. And he handed the lobster rolls out.

Perkins sat down again and bit off half of his.

I pushed mine away.

\* \* \*

Rosselli's tale had been too much. I had learned only that he got angry at the mention of gambling on Tour, no real details. I went to a cherry bookshelf, admiring the leather-bound editions. I found a version of Shakespeare's complete works and pawed through it, stopping at "The Phoenix and The Turtle." The poem's opening line read:

*eLt the loudest bird of lay,...*

Sometimes my dyslexic fits come out of nowhere. Many dyslexics never develop ways to cope. In those cases, the results are never good. At a fundraiser, a guy from the Orton Society, a national dyslexic organization, once told me it was feared prisons held many undiagnosed dyslexics. I studied the poem again:

> *Let the bird of loudest lay,*
> *On the sole Arabian tree,*
> *Herald sad and trumpet be,*
> *To whose sound chaste wings obey.*
>
> *But thou, shrieking harbinger,*
> *Foul precurrer of the fiend,*
> *Augur of the fever's end,*
> *To this troop come thou not near!*

Beat you again, dyslexia. "To this troop come thou not near!" I was already in the middle of the troop. Sorry, Shakespeare.

"Jack, been looking for you." It was troop leader Frank Rosselli, standing alone behind me. "Need to talk serious for a minute."

\* \* \*

"I've been considering what you said about needing money," Rosselli was sitting behind a large cherry desk in an office off the main room. I sat across from him in a leather chair.

His hands rested atop three sheets of paper on a green desk blotter.

"You need money and I need a partner," he said.

I leaned back. Now I knew why he'd told me the story about the .44 Magnum. It had been a test. My gut reaction had been quick and disgusted—which was why he'd been pleased. He figured I was frightened and, thus, wouldn't betray him. He had mistaken disgust for frightened. But he didn't need to know that.

"A partner?" I said.

"What do you know about betting on the Tour?" he said.

"What did you have in mind?" I said. A partnership in a gambling ring meant *I'd* be throwing strokes. That didn't jive with Hutch's scenario. Hutch was no one's partner, and if he'd been responsible for Hutch's blackmail, why not simply continue with that venture?

"Tell me what you know," he said, "so I have a place to start."

"I don't know anything."

There was a wet bar on the far wall. He said: "Jack, mix me a drink, please."

"I don't work for you."

He leaned forward. "People do what I say."

I had helped him hustle someone; I had listened to his story about killing a guy in cold blood; my dyslexia was acting up; and I was tired. I was in no mood to wait on him.

"You going to get that fucking drink?" He stood up.

In hindsight, maybe I should've just gotten the damned drink. I knew he liked thinking I feared him. But enough was enough. I stood up across from him.

We stared at each other for about five seconds.

A broad smile broke across his face. "Tommy would've run over and made the drink. Takes balls. I like that."

I didn't say anything. He wasn't easy to figure out. He had just contradicted himself.

He moved from behind the desk to the wet bar and poured two drinks. As he worked, I glanced at the papers on the desk and saw several names next to numbers. In the middle of the list, I saw my name with 1-250 next to it.

Rosselli brought me a Scotch. He leaned back in his chair and put his feet on the blotter near the papers.

—

"I'm looking for a business partner who plays on Tour," he said. "The guy currently running things used to have what it takes."

"Which is?"

"Balls and brains. When I got into the action, he was the man. Now he's old and tired."

He sipped some scotch. "I'll keep the old man around—I've made a lot of money betting against him, though I lost my fucking shirt this season." He smiled. "So far, that is. Anyway, me and him both know I run the show now."

One name came to mind: Pickorino.

"What exactly is 'the show'?" I said.

"Taking what the oddsmakers give you and making money."

I glanced at the sheets of paper again.

He took the papers, folded them, and set them on the desk. He had liked thinking I feared him; then he liked me standing up to him. Now he didn't trust me. "There are odds on everything," he said. "Including golf tournaments."

I'd learned that via the Internet. I wished I'd had my recorder. We were getting some place now.

"Like today. We won the front, back, and total strokes, but I made more on side bets."

"First on, first in?"

"Yeah."

"I'd like to know about the entire operation," I said, "see how it all works."

He studied me.

I took a chance: "I'm careful," I said. "If I'm getting involved, I want to know all about it."

"There's nothing to see, which is why it works. What did you expect, table dancers and dice in my suite? No computers, no nothing. The old man has a partner—a guy owns a casino in Vegas—it all works through him. Sometimes I go right through Joh—" He looked up to see if I'd picked up on Pickorino's name.

I played dumb.

"Now the casino owner's branching out," I said, "taking side bets?"

"Yeah. If I had someone—"

The office door flew open and Gianni ran in waving my tape recorder and pointing at me. "You fucking rat. All the money I give you for coming and you try—" Gianni pulled a gun from his belt in a frantic jerk.

I dove to the floor and was around the side of the desk.

"Tommy!" Rosselli was on his feet. "What's going on? Put that away."

"Franky, he's a rat. A fucking, stinking rat." Now Gianni was waving the recorder in one hand, the gun in the other.

"Give me the gun, Tommy," Frank said. "The place is full of people. I told you to quit that fucking coke. It makes you jumpy. Give me the gun."

Gianni opened his mouth to protest, then closed it.

I saw him hand the pistol over and I came out. It's hard to come out from beneath a desk in a dignified manner, but I did my best.

"Give me that." Rosselli took the recorder and pointed to the chair. I sat again. He hit play.

The tape replayed me asking Rosselli the question about money, to which his reply had ultimately been a threat. As it replayed, he glared at me, the crazed look I'd seen now high voltage.

"What's the problem?" I said.

"You're a fucking snitch," Gianni said. His voice was shrill.

"What the fuck is going on?" I said. "This is bullshit. I'm here to play golf and win. We did. You don't trust me, don't invite me. But don't send your weaklings to go through my stuff, Frank." It was the best I had.

Rosselli stood looking at me.

"Rewind the tape to the beginning," I said.

No one moved.

"Rewind it."

Rosselli eyed me, then Gianni, who stood smiling as if this was his biggest accomplishment. Rosselli rewound the tape to the beginning—and my backup plan. My voice played loud and clear:

*"Today is January third. I shot 67 in Vero Beach, Florida. I hit six of 14 fairways and need to work on driving accuracy. I needed only 25 putts, which is encouraging. My swing lacked rhythm, so I should practice with a pitching wedge and hit some bunker shots to make myself use a long flowing swing."*

Rosselli glared at me and paused the tape.

"He," I motioned my head to Gianni, "took that out of my golf bag. I use that for notes after I play. I keep it in the pocket of my golf bag. Sometimes it gets jarred and begins recording."

"For notes?" Gianni said. "Notes on what?"

"Small Boy," Frank said, "I'll handle this. Explain."

"I just did. I'm dyslexic. Instead of writing things down, I tape myself. I learn via audio." I was fairly sure he didn't care which learning style best fit my needs, but I went with it.

"So you make notes about how you played and what to work on?" Frank said.

"Yeah. I've got tapes going back 20 years. I started doing it at 15."

"I'll keep this tape," he said.

"Fine."

"O.K. Tommy, stop going through Jack's things. You were supposed to have checked him thoroughly before the round. Did you?"

"Of course."

"Come here," Frank said.

Gianni moved closer to him and Rosselli examined Gianni's face.

"Tommy, there's blow on your nose."

"What?"

"Exactly. Don't lie to me."

Gianni said nothing.

"We don't mix business and pleasure." Rosselli slapped Gianni's face again. This time the slap was a full swing and dropped Gianni to his knees. Rosselli hit him again with the back of his hand.

Gianni sat kneeling, stunned.

Rosselli grabbed him by his tie, hoisted him to his feet. "I've taken care of you your whole life and you break my one rule." He shoved Gianni hard and the little man went to the door in a rush before regaining his footing. He stopped and looked back at Rosselli for a long time. Then he walked out.

"I believe you, Jack. But just so you know how things work, let me tell you what would've happened had you been taping me."

I reached for my Scotch.

"You would've been driven to the middle of the desert, shot in the kneecaps, left for 20 minutes, then had each arm severed, left like that for 20 minutes — you can see where this is going."

"Fun in the sun."

He smiled. "It's good to have a sense of humor, but that can only take a guy so far."

"I was under the desk, Frank."

"That's Tommy. I am no cokehead."

The clock on the wall read 3:30. I had been with him long enough. "What did you have in mind before he came in? I assume we're talking a fix."

"Yeah."

I had no recorder. There was no sense in going further. "O.K.," I said. "It's been a long day. I'm in, but let's work out the details later."

# Chapter Sixteen

———

LISA AND I HAD DECIDED on La Casa Sena in Santa Fe for dinner. Actually, I had to talk her into it. She was tired and said she wanted to stay in Albuquerque and have room service.

She was very quiet during the hour-long drive. In fact, she had said very little since we'd left her house in Maryland.

With black jeans and boots, she had on a thick black sweater. I was dressed casually preppy in blue jeans, loafers, and a blue button-down. The ride up Route 25 to Santa Fe was always spectacular. The landscape makes you think you've stepped into a Coors commercial. And the drive is simple—usually. This night, however, I got lost. Once in Santa Fe, I could picture the entire downtown area, and knew precisely where I had to go, but I couldn't envision how to get there. It had happened many times before, even in cities or towns I knew well. Getting lost remained the single most frustrating aspect of dyslexia for me. In some cases, it occurred after taking the exact same route only one day earlier. On this night, it set the tone for the meal.

\* \* \*

In La Casa Sena, I pulled Lisa's chair out for her.

"This place is great," I said.

The inside of La Casa Sena was blonde—bar top, tables, and hardwood floors. The walls and ceiling, which was lined with huge beams, were adobe. There was a brick fireplace near the bar and a

———

piano in the middle of the room. Our waitress was tiny with big green eyes. She wore black pants, a formfitting white shirt, and, as it would turn out, had a voice to die for. She took our drink orders, then, before going to the bar, took the pianist's cue, and broke into the theme from *Evita*. Madonna would have been envious.

As she sang, the lights dimmed, and a spotlight fell near the piano. The room went silent. I watched Lisa and tried to remember her looking tired before. I couldn't. I knew she was working her job covering weekly Tour events; and that she was still on the Hutch Gainer story—I knew that because she hadn't mentioned it. I didn't like seeing her tired. I didn't like knowing she was frustrated with me. But, as I'd told her, I couldn't remain the man I was—the man she'd fallen in love with—if I simply turned my back on this.

When the song was done, our waitress returned with drinks. I had Red Hook Ale; Lisa, a glass of chardonnay.

"Great voice," I said.

"Thank you." She smiled broadly. "I just started here."

"Where are you from?" Lisa said.

"Woodstock, New York. I was doing off-Broadway for a while. Now I'm going to UNM and living here."

After we ordered, the waitress said to me: "Thanks again for the compliment," and smiled at me before leaving.

Lisa said something under her breath and watched her go.

We were quiet for a while. The silence was not comfortable.

"How often do you get like you were in the car?" she said.

"Mad? It's not like I got out, yelled, and picked a fight. I just swore once. It's frustrating."

"Why not ask for directions?"

"Because usually I'm very close to where I want to go."

"It took us 30 minutes from the exit, Jack."

"So this time I wasn't as close."

"Should've asked."

"You haven't spoken to me all evening," I said. "But you start a conversation with the waitress, though."

She leaned forward and rested her elbows on the tabletop. "Then let's talk. Let's talk about Hutch Gainer. Let's talk about gambling on Tour. Let's talk about Hutch's stroke-per-round average rising almost two shots since he won."

I managed not to fall out of my seat—but just barely. She was hot on the trail.

The lights died again and a waiter stood next to the piano and sang something I couldn't name but knew was from *Phantom of the Opera*. I was thankful for the interruption. Our waitress returned, leaned close to me, and asked if I'd like another beer. Seemed rude to say no. And it was Red Hook Ale. And, at 215 pounds I could have two or three. And most importantly, Lisa knew something about Hutch. I said yes and managed not to say *hell* yes. She smiled at me again and left.

When the song was done, I sat sipping my second beer, and waited.

"She's attractive," Lisa said, "isn't she?"

"Cute but young."

I kept looking at Lisa as I drank, then I said: "I hate this. I was an ass in the car, but that has nothing to do with it."

"No, it doesn't. We're supposed to be getting married and you're involved in something dangerous."

"You've said 'supposed to' twice now."

We were silent. I had some beer. Lisa examined the other tables. Many people were tourists, dressed casually. Probably up from California or in from Denver.

She turned back to me. "Twice?"

"Yeah. Want to talk about it?"

"I'm scared. I'm mad. I'm insulted. I'm hurt."

"Because I can't tell you what's going on with Hutch Gainer."

"Because you *won't*."

The cute but young waitress brought our meals. I had the chicken fried steak. Lisa had something that looked like a cross between salad and lasagna.

"I'm flying to Houston with your golf partner, Frank Rosselli," Lisa said.

"Don't do that."

"Why?"

"Don't do it."

"And why not?" she said. "Is he dangerous? How'd your corporate outing go?"

I kept chewing.

"I spoke with him on the phone." She took a bite and swallowed. "It's funny. Houston OCU says when he was in high school, Rosselli got his start as a bookie."

"You called the Organized Crime Unit?"

"Want to talk about Hutch's stroke average?"

The waitress returned again. "Are you Mr. Austin?"

"Yes."

"You have a phone call from a Mr. Perkins. He says it's urgent."

\* \* \*

I relayed what Perkins had said to Lisa: John Pickorino had been murdered; Hutch Gainer was being held and that his prints were on the murder weapon—a 9 mm Smith & Wesson. We took our doggy-bagged dinners and headed back to Albuquerque.

There wasn't anything to say anymore. So we drove in silence. The speed limit was 75; I had the Buick courtesy car at 85 most of the way down Route 25. We went directly to the downtown Albuquerque police station.

From her expression, I knew her mind was going a mile a minute. Mine raced as well: at my welcome-back party, Hutch had moved in a fog of depression; in the hospital, he had called and there had been desperation in his voice; and he had realized— seemingly during our phone conversation—that if Pickorino was gone, he'd be free.

\* \* \*

Perkins greeted us inside the station. Lisa, locating her CBS affiliate, said nothing and went right to work.

Perkins and I sat in a row of chairs along a wall across from the front desk. Cops moved to and fro, as if to the clacking of shoes on linoleum tiles. The place had a dingy, stale odor. The people who weren't cops looked hard or defeated. But none looked scared.

"They've got him out back with his court-appointed lawyer," Perkins said.

"He's been charged?" I said.

"Yeah," Perkins said. "About 8:30, I went to the lobby. Cops were everywhere. Someone said a guy'd been shot. So I went look-ing for the room—up to the fifth floor. Chee was there, let me in. Pickorino was dead. Shot once in the chest. They found the gun across the hall in Hutch's things."

"That's convenient."

\* \* \*

I was thinking of a line in *King Lear* where Kent says, "I have a journey, sir, shortly to go; / My master calls me, I must not say no" and relating it to my recent ongoings. Perkins had gone to talk shop with some cops. And then I realized how lucky I had been to have been the victim, tucked away in my cozy hospital room, when I'd been assaulted.

I made this realization when three guys came running over to me. One was in a blue suit; the others wore jeans. The jean gang looked sloppy: one guy had on a disheveled and unbuttoned shirt over a T-shirt; his cohort wore a gray sweatshirt with what looked like a pink Kool-Aid stain near the collar. Both wore baseball hats that said ESPN. One of them held a camera.

Suit said: "Jack Austin."

I know how tough journalism can be and, to that point, had never declined an interview. But this time I knew I couldn't say anything. I tried to explain that, but they wouldn't take no. The third time I declined they put the camera on me.

The guy with the microphone smiled. The red light on the camera went on and a spotlight beam nearly blinded me.

"I'm here with Jack Austin. What can you tell us, Jack?"

"Nothing," I said.

"What do you know about what happened?"

"Not a thing," I said.

"Can you describe the players' emotions?"

"No."

"How well do you know Hutch Gainer?"

My attempt at boring had failed, so I began listing every sports cliché I'd ever heard: "I owe everything to my parents."

"What about the murder of John Pickorino?"

"We're one big happy family."

"Are you here in support of Hutch Gainer, who is charged with first-degree murder?"

"I'm just glad to be here."

"Did you sense anything leading up to this?"

"Golf's a crazy game."

"You played with Hutch recently. How was he acting?"

"It's all about winning."

Suit nodded, catching on. "Is there anything you can tell us about the murder?"

"If we work as a team, God willing, we can overcome this."

"Is that it?"

"Winning isn't everything; it's the *only* thing."

Finally, he shook his head.

"I'm just glad I could contribute," I said.

Over the next two hours, CNN, the *Dallas Morning News*, the

*LA Times*, and the Golf Channel appeared. I didn't see Lisa. I asked a CBS colleague where she was. It was a young college kid working as an intern.

"She's amazing," he said. "Such a pro. She had someone from wardrobe come over, changed in the bathroom, taped a 30-second recap then headed back to the hotel. Said everyone else had this story already and didn't want to just repeat facts."

I thanked the young intern. Lisa was working the story from another angle. I thought about that for a long while.

# Chapter Seventeen

———

AT 11:30, PERKINS AND I were told Hutch's court-appointed attorney had asked to see me. A stone-faced officer walked us down a corridor and stopped in front of a large steel door with no window. Inside, Hutch sat looking like a man already sentenced to death. He was pale and there were dark rings around his eyes. He wore a white T-shirt, blue jeans, and boots. There were sweat stains at his armpits.

A tall gaunt man with a thick moustache, slacks and a crisp white shirt stood and shook my hand. "Gerry Smythe," the lawyer said. "A doctor's coming in later. Hutch is having stomach pains."

I told him who I was and introduced Perkins. Smythe reclaimed the seat across a metal table from Hutch. Perkins and I remained standing.

"Hutch, what happened?" I said. "A man is dead."

"I walked in and he's on the floor—"

"Hutch," Smythe said, "you don't need to answer that again." Then to me: "I can explain later."

"They're O.K." Hutch said. "I was coming back from dinner— I told Johnny I needed to stretch, so I went for a walk. When I came back, the door was open. There was blood everywhere—his chest, his neck. I start yelling and a maid runs in and she starts screaming. And it's like chaos. And then cops were there. Everything happened fast."

"You were staying across the hall or in some other room, right?" I said.

"How'd you know that?"

"Because Jenna's in town this week."

"Yeah. Right. She was with Pickorino. So I had my own room."

I wondered how she got away from Pickorino long enough to two-time him.

"Who's Jenna?" Smythe said.

"Where was Kiko?" I said.

"He had a room down the hall. Probably there."

"Pickorino was alone?" Perkins said. "That worked out well for somebody."

"Where was Jenna when this happened?" I said.

"I don't know."

"This isn't an interrogation," Smythe said.

"He's"—Hutch pointed at Perkins—"working for me."

"In what capacity? " Smythe said.

Hutch ignored that.

I said: "You did not shoot him?"

"Jesus Christ," Hutch said, "what do you think I am?"

"A confused and very desperate kid. When I was in the hospital, over the phone you said if Pickorino was out of the picture, your problems were solved."

"Hey," Smythe said, "what's going on? What problems?"

Hutch gazed at each of us, one at a time. Then his eyes locked on mine. The air in the room was stale and smelled of sweat. A man was possibly facing execution if convicted. And he had all the motive in the world and apparently no alibi.

"Jesus—Jack, Perkins—you guys are all I got. You got to believe me."

"They found the gun in your room," Perkins said. "That would be pretty stupid, but I don't take you for smart to begin with."

"Hey," Smythe said. "Don't insult my client."

"You were scared, felt guilty, and walked in there and ended the blackmail once and for all," Perkins said.

"No." Hutch was on the edge of his chair now. "No, I didn't."

"Blackmail?" Smythe said. "What is going on, Hutch? I need to know—"

Perkins slammed his huge palm on the table. The blow of the flat hand echoed like a gun shot in an empty gymnasium. Smythe shut up and Hutch flinched. So did I.

"Hutch, I'm off the case. You killed a man tonight. Admit it to me and it goes no further."

"I didn't do it, man." Hutch looked frantically from Perkins to me. "Jack—man—you guys got to believe me. I didn't do it."

I said nothing.

"Hey, look, like, I've done things—hustled, threw some strokes, but I'm no killer. Why would I have waited this long? Look at me. I'm a wreck. Can't sleep. My stomach's a mess."

"Exactly," I said. "You're a mess. So you took matters—"

Hutch stood up and pointed at me ready to fight. "No, goddamn it. No. I've done a lot I shouldn't have, but not this. I'm no killer."

* * *

The bar was poorly lit; the floor was lathered with a dirt and beer combination that smelled like it had been there since Ben Hogan played, and the barkeep was slow and made no conversation. But I had called Chee and told him I wanted to talk. He had said he was off duty and picked this place.

I wanted to know where Jenna had been when Pickorino was shot.

At a couple minutes before 1:00 A.M. I got a cup of black coffee and Perkins took a draft and a shot of Jack Daniels, and we sat across from Chee in a booth.

"So you ready to talk, Jack?" He wasn't smoking, but there was a littered ashtray.

"Hutch didn't do it," I said.

"His prints were on the gun. And the gun was in his sock drawer."

"That how you catch most of your murderers?" I said.

"He isn't your typical murderer." Chee drank from a draft. "Doesn't know what he's doing."

"A little scotchtape," Perkins said, "and anyone can lift prints."

"Anyone can," Chee said. "The question is why anyone would."

The bartender set a plate of burritos, refried beans, and Spanish rice in front of Chee.

"Dinner of champions," I said.

"I was at home," Chee said.

"Dinner's on me," Perkins said, then to the bartender: "Start a tab."

"Thanks," Chee said. "So, Jack, what have you got?"

I sipped my coffee and thought about what I knew: gambling, spawned from a casino in Vegas, was occurring on and at PGA Tour events; Rosselli wanted me to be his on-course partner; Hutch was being blackmailed and had thrown strokes. I set my coffee down.

Chee sat very still, one thick hand resting around a beer glass, the other holding a fork. His dark, penetrating eyes stared into mine.

"I've got to have your word whatever I say doesn't leave this booth?" I said.

He shook his head. "No way."

"I'm not confessing a murder," I said. "And I don't know who did."

"What then?"

Through a doorway, I heard the sound of pool balls being struck, then a holler.

"What do you have," Chee said, "that can't leave this booth?"

I looked at him. He knew I wanted his word.

"Off the damned record," he said.

I told him all of it.

Halfway through it, the bartender brought me more coffee and a fresh draft and shot for Perkins; Chee finished his late dinner by the time I had completed my reprise.

"Schilling ought to know," Chee said.

"No way. That's why we're here. You, I trust. Him, I do not. You gave me your word what I said would stay here."

"It will. So the assault was a warning?"

"You go public with this and it could cost me my life," I said. Chee wouldn't care about me trying to keep a potential scandal out of the press, so I had to use a different—but equally important —angle.

He sat staring at me. Then he said: "How much time do you want? I need to act on this, Jack. It's my job."

"Let me meet with Frank," I said.

"And set up a sting? I need to go to my superiors for that."

"Not a sting. Let's just see what develops."

"I can't wait forever, but I'll keep my word."

"It won't be forever," I said and leaned back, tired from thinking about it all.

* * *

A half hour after closing, Chee was leaning against the wall with his legs stretched out on the seat of the booth. The pool players had left; the bartender was sitting on a stool behind the bar, watching a late-night talk show. He obviously knew Chee was a cop, so I figured we were welcome to stay.

"Rosselli said he had no problem with Pickorino because he

won a lot of money from him," Chee said.

"But he said lately he'd been losing his shirt," I said.

"So he wasn't blackmailing Gainer."

"That line may've been a cover," Perkins said. He had gotten a chair from a table and was sitting in it, his feet splayed before him, his arms folded across his chest.

"But," I said, "Rosselli's seeing Pickorino's girlfriend, Jenna."

"The blonde?" Chee said.

"Yeah. Where were she and Kiko when Pickorino was shot?" I said.

"She was down in the fitness room. Got a witness and her signature on the sign-in book."

"And Kiko?" Perkins said.

"Having dinner with his aunt. Nice old lady—wears a hearing aid and glasses thick as two-by-fours. I went to see her myself. But, we didn't know about Jenna and Rosselli. Hold on."

Chee went to the bar and used the phone. After the call, he returned. "Someone'll stake out Jenna tonight and grab her tomorrow at eight A.M. and bring her in. I'll have a little chat with her. Guys at the station said Schilling was looking for me."

I smiled.

"He's a pain in the ass," Chee said.

Perkins grinned.

"So," Chee said, "we've got: Hutch Gainer being blackmailed to play like crap; Pickorino serving as Hutch's sponsor; Rosselli and Pickorino banging the same lady and gambling on the same thing; and you becoming a mob partner, Jack."

I hesitated, then shrugged. "Yeah."

"Jealousy can lead to murder," Perkins said.

Chee drank some beer. "Especially when we're talking about two guys who find it easy to do."

"But Rosselli said he won a lot from Pickorino," I said. "Would he kill Pickorino and lose that source of income?"

"You said he was losing right now."

"Yeah, but that only started recently."

"This job gets easier with each passing day," Chee said. He took another sip and grinned. "You miss it?" he said to Perkins.

"I'm still in it."

"But you get to choose which cases you take."

Perkins's stare ran to me. "Usually."

"I'll buy the next round," I said.

# Chapter Eighteen

---

On Tour, Wednesday is a practice day—Hutch Gainer crisis or not. And I was on the driving range, slowed by a nasty headache, at 8:30. The sun could be seen above a distant mesa, and the clack of clubheads striking range balls was like birdsong after the previous night. Between gulps of black coffee, I hit maybe a hundred balls in two hours. I then changed into shorts and a T-shirt, and went to the Tour's 48-foot fitness trailer.

Padre was riding a stationary bike and Grant Ashley was doing dumbbell bench presses with 35-pound hand weights.

"Need help with those?" I said.

"Low weight, high reps," Grant said. His Southern drawl dragged 'reps' to three syllables.

"Raps?" I said.

"Reps." He set the weight down and gave me the finger.

"Learn to speak Yankee," I said.

Padre chuckled. "You going to do anything besides aggravate people?"

"I'm playing to my strength," I said.

"Annoyance?" he said.

I did some push-ups, then rolled onto my back and did slow sit-ups for 15 minutes. Then I moved to a bench and did presses with hundred-pound dumbbells in each hand. I did four sets of 15, then flies with 45s, and military presses with 75s. As we worked out, the TV was tuned to The Golf Channel and we watched the European Tour. I wasn't familiar with the event, but Lee

---

Westwood was leading by two over Berhard Langer. Monty was in third.

I was doing seated curls with 50-pound dumbbells when Grant said, "What's this?" He was standing, clicker in hand, before the TV.

The screen said CBS and BREAKING NEWS. Lisa was near the 18th green outside the fitness trailer. She wore a cream-colored skirt suit and held a microphone in one hand, a note pad in the other.

"What's going on?" I set the weights down and stood next to Grant and Padre near the TV. Several other players came over.

When the camera zoomed in, Lisa said: "Hutch Gainer, charged last night with the first-degree murder of his sponsor, John Pickorino, may have been throwing strokes during PGA Tour events as part of a gambling operation."

"Holy Mother," Padre said.

"Throwing strokes?" Grant said.

"What's she talking about, Jack?" a voice behind me said.

"I don't know." All eyes were on me.

There was a shot of the hotel, then Pickorino's room—complete with yellow crime-scene tape across the door. Then Lisa again: "Pickorino was an organized crime figure in New Orleans, according to New Orleans Police Spokesman Jerry O'Neill, and the leader of a Mafia family. After winning twice earlier this season, Hutch Gainer's play declined steadily, leading to questions regarding his association with Pickorino. CBS Sports has obtained evidence from former FBI agent and current Head of Tour Security Tom Schilling, which suggests Gainer was teaming with Pickorino to fix illegal bets on tournaments..."

My head began to throb. She had worded it carefully. She wasn't right—he wasn't working with Pickorino; he had been black-mailed. But she wasn't entirely wrong—he had intentionally screwed up holes.

"That fucker," Grant said.

"They better ban him," someone said.

"He ought to do time."

Padre said: "Let's not jump to conclusions. Jack, what evidence does she have?"

"I don't know. I haven't seen her since dinner last night."

The van fell silent, and I knew not many people believed me.

On the screen, Lisa was holding up a paper. The camera zoomed in.

It was a list of players and odds.

"This is what is used to gamble legally in Las Vegas or overseas," she said.

Then she held up a different sheet. It was like the first one, except many handwritten notes were in the margins.

"This document was found in John Pickorino's room last night by Head of Tour Security Tom Schilling. Next to the odds, there are side bets listed, such as who might bogey a particular hole. Hutch Gainer is listed to bogey the par-five 15th. Last week, he did in fact bogey that hole each day."

Padre pursed his lips and said nothing.

"Gainer's attorney refused to comment," Lisa said. "CBS Sports will continue to follow this story and will continue to be the leader in bringing you breaking news."

And then we were staring at the European Tour again. And all eyes were still on me.

I wondered if it was too late to apply for a European Tour card.

* * *

"Thing is," Chee said, "that sheet of paper might not hold up in court."

Chee, Perkins, and I sat at the bar in the hotel restaurant. It was busy. Hutch Gainer's arrest had been good for business. Reporters had descended upon Albuquerque like paratroopers. They sat around tables in teams—camera jockeys dressed casually, eating and chatting with someone in a suit, doubtless the TV personality. They read newspapers and watched the TV above the bar, probably leery of another breaking news segment by Lisa, who had scooped everyone with her evidence piece. Unfortunately, I was one of the scoopees—Perkins, Chee, and I never saw it coming.

I had just ordered a foot-long tuna, Swiss cheese, onions, and mayo sandwich, and was drinking water. Chee had ordered quasadillas and coffee. Perkins was having a BLT and a draft beer.

"Schilling waited for me last night," Chee said. "I was in the bar with you two. Then I went home to sleep a few hours. He went back to the hotel, flashed his outdated FBI credentials. Got in the room."

"Your boss must love that," Perkins said. "Head of the caddie shack snooping around the crime scene."

"Loves it," Chee said. "And not only tampering with evidence, but taking it. Then giving it to a reporter?" Chee shook his head.

"He'll be at the department answering questions for a while."

"How'd your guys miss that sheet?" I said.

"Cops are overworked," Perkins said.

"It was hidden pretty well," Chee said. "It's no excuse, but—"

"Who's handling the investigation?" I said.

"Me."

"So, why aren't you questioning Schilling?"

"He's got a stake in this," Chee said. "I won't deny him that, but I got him answering to a couple really tough cops he doesn't know. He asked to see me three times before I left to meet you." He grinned, a devilish smile.

"Any defense attorney will use Schilling's stunt to prove how inept your department is," Perkins said. "Might even get the odds sheet thrown out."

Chee shook his head. "No way."

"Why would he give it to Lisa?" I said. "He's the type to hold his own press conference, be a hero."

"That's what they're asking her."

"Her?" I said.

The bartender set our lunches down.

Chee said: "She was in possession of a sheet of paper, which is evidence taken from the crime scene. Both were answering questions when I left—she's with Schilling in this."

"How long has she been down there?" I said.

"You didn't know she'd been called in?"

"No," I said.

We ate in silence for a while. His question made me think. She was my fiancée. Now she sat—I assumed terrified—in a police station, being grilled by tough cops.

Chee must've seen something in my face. "For what it's worth, I don't see her being arrested. And she'll be out soon."

I exhaled.

"But I'm impressed that she got a slimeball like Schilling to give her that sheet of paper. There's a lot of other reporters out there he could've given it to. Or why not keep it himself?"

I didn't like Schilling; I didn't like the way he looked at Lisa.

I told Perkins I was going to find her, dropped some bills on the bar, and started out the door—just as Lisa walked in.

* * *

She was still wearing the cream skirt, matching blazer, and

heels she had worn during her breaking-news feature. She had on sunglasses now and moved slowly to a booth.

I sat across from her.

With her left hand, she took off the glasses.

Her eyes were bloodshot, but that wasn't what I noticed first. As I stared at her bare left hand, I felt a balloon of fire swell inside my chest. But I didn't mention it. When we feel guilty about the pain we cause others, sometimes we make light of it. "You've really got things stirred up around here."

A waiter came over and she ordered a salad and a Diet Coke.

"It's my job to break stories, Jack."

"Hutch didn't kill him."

Her forearms rested atop the table. "That's not for me to decide."

"You've painted a pretty clear picture for the public, though."

"I present the story. The public draws its own conclusion."

I leaned back and folded my arms. "It's like writing *police will neither confirm nor deny*. You're suggesting it."

"He was goddamned arrested, Jack."

The waiter returned with her Diet Coke and said her salad would be right out.

"You should've waited to see what develops."

"Be realistic," she said, "just for one second."

"I am."

"No, you're not. And you haven't been. I've known something was going on since you got hurt and Pickorino came to the hospital. Then I found out Hutch came to our suite. Next, Rosselli shows up at my house. I do some research and find Hutch's stroke average has risen significantly almost overnight."

"That doesn't mean he killed anyone."

"And I didn't say he did. The cops said that. When I got the odds sheet, I looked at Hutch's final round last week. Somebody bet Hutch would bogey the 18th hole. He did. My guess is Pickorino bet he'd do it and cut Hutch in on the profits. I can put two and two together."

She had done a lot of work on this story. And she had done nothing amoral. But she didn't know about the blackmail.

Rosselli had said he'd lost money to Pickorino this season. If he were fixing golf rounds, he'd be winning. And Pickorino, with his man vs. man talk in my hospital room, seemed like a purist. It didn't sound like he would fix the outcome either.

"And I could've gone with something a lot earlier," she said.

---

"Said your assault was suspicious and that authorities would *neither confirm nor deny* if the assault had anything to do with noted mobsters John Pickorino and/or Frank Rosselli having appeared in galleries at Tour events recently. That would be planting a seed of suspicion. I didn't do that."

The waiter brought her salad.

"What I want to know, Jack, is why would Hutch murder his business partner?"

"He didn't do it."

"He was throwing strokes."

"Do you know that?" I said.

"You do."

I shook my head. I didn't owe Hutch a thing. He had gotten me beaten up and had disrupted my season. Yet I had seen a look in his eyes and heard something in his voice in that jail cell that made me believe him. However, the stroke throwing was now a full-blown scandal; I hadn't stopped that, just delayed it. And the person who had not allowed my goal to be fulfilled sat across from me.

Her bare left hand was in front of her face. "Where's the engagement ring?" I said.

"I took it off last night. Must've forgot to put it back on."

"Why'd you take it off? How'd you get the paper from Schilling?"

"What?"

"How'd you get the paper from Schilling? I don't like the way he looks at you." The words were coming faster than my mind comprehended them. I was tired and frustrated.

"Are you nuts? We're too old for jealous fits, Jack."

"He just gave you the paper? You took the ring off."

"What are you saying?" she said. "That I slept with Schilling to get the paper?"

I didn't speak and looked away. When my eyes went back to her, she was crying.

"Don't you know me better than that?"

I did, but didn't say it.

"I took the ring off last night because I'm not sure anymore, Jack."

Her face was in conflict—fear, then anger, then anguish.

She took a deep breath. "I know Schilling expects something in return. He'll never get it. If you think I'd do that, then you never knew me."

The tears streamed down her cheeks now.

I had to look away.

"You haven't trusted me with this since day one," she said.

"I tried to keep you out of it."

"Why?"

I shook my head.

"We're in two single-minded professions, Jack. Maybe the careers are too much."

She dropped her head into her hands and cried. She was as tough a person as I had known. Something seemed to grab the pit of my stomach and squeeze. I didn't know what to say.

We sat like that for an eternity.

Then she looked up. "I'd like to be alone."

"Lisa, I didn't mean—"

"I'd be happier if you weren't here right now."

"O.K." I left the bar.

# Chapter Nineteen

———

At least Rosselli was smart—I had to give him that; he didn't take a chance on us being seen together. The previous night had been long and the conversation with Lisa had made me even more tired. I had gotten a late start on the day, but had to practice. So I went to the hotel lot, where my Buick courtesy car was parked, to head to the course.

I never made it.

As I went to unlock my door, a huge black Suburban pulled into the slot next to my car. And, under the midday sun, Rosselli, wearing black Raybans and a white Ashworth shirt with blue stripes, got out. The parking lot was full of cars, but not many people. I knew most players were already at the club.

"Hell of a way to schedule a meeting," I said.

"You said we'd work out the details later. Now is later."

"I'm headed to the course."

He shook his head in a gesture which illustrated his sense of power.

I ignored his sense of power. "Yeah," I said, "I'm going to practice."

"Your fiancée's story bothers me. Now get in my car."

\* \* \*

Albuquerque is not a small town. I didn't know where we were heading. Frank and I sat in the third seat; Gianni drove and the brown-haired *GQ* cover boy, Joey Chrissani, who'd been in the clubhouse after our golf outing, sat next to him. Neither of them spoke and no radio played.

"How much does she know?" Frank said.

"I don't know."

"What do you mean you don't know?"

"I'm about to get involved in this, Frank. I don't bring the topic up."

"You separate business from family," he said. "That's smart. I've always done that."

Joey Chrissani sat looking out the window disinterested, like people I'd seen on airplanes; occasionally Gianni's eyes flashed in the rearview mirror.

"Let's get down to business," Frank said. "I picked you because you fit what I was looking for better than anyone else."

"Which is?"

"You've played a long time, so you know the game and the Tour. But you're not too successful."

I ran my tongue along my upper teeth and exhaled.

"And you don't have so much money that money doesn't matter. And, given your relationship, you've got access to privileged information."

He didn't know Lisa was no longer wearing my ring.

"You involved with that sheet of paper Lisa got from Schilling?" I said.

He looked at me appraisingly. They had sat waiting for me to emerge from the hotel. They had caught me alone, which I guessed had been the point. Now his eyes glanced over my shirt. I had on only a red shirt with blue stripes and khaki pants—no jacket or sweater or anything under which one could hide a mic.

"I'm involved," he said. "Pickorino thought he was running the show. Now he's out of the picture."

"I thought you said you weren't going to take him out."

He looked at me the way he had on the golf course, when he had all but threatened my life. I caught Gianni's eyes in the rearview mirror; Joey was watching traffic go by.

"Jack," Frank shook his head, "you got balls."

"Business partners speak candidly, don't they?"

"Not in my business. It's good for you that I didn't have him clipped."

"You think Hutch Gainer did it?"

"I don't give a fuck. I made money off Pickorino. Not this

year, but I made money. It was enjoyable with him, though. He was determined and I liked that. Now it'll be an income-generating enterprise only."

"I want to know the entire operation if I'm getting involved."

He looked me over carefully. "Giacomin has a bookie in Vegas who'll cover large bets."

"You trust Giacomin and his bookie?"

"The bookie operates strictly in big money. Has for years."

"How big?"

"I put a million on Fred Couples once."

"But we're focusing on side bets."

"Yeah. Obviously, we can't do it every week, but when we hit, it'll be big."

"The bookie takes side bets."

"This one does."

"Does Giacomin have contact with any Tour players?"

Rosselli tilted his head. "Why do you ask?"

"What if he's doing the same thing we are?"

"Who gives a fuck? He doesn't have the money I have. So he won't make what we will."

"Who else bets?"

"Bunch of guys. If you can cover the minimum bet, you can play."

"What's the minimum?"

"Two-fifty."

"I take it you left off some zeros?"

From the front of the truck, Gianni said: "What do you think, Jack? I don't like him asking questions, Frank."

"I know that, Small Boy," Frank said. "You don't like it because you don't do it. Jack's careful. We'll show Jack the consequences of," he paused and thought of the best way to phrase it, "misusing my trust."

* * *

We had driven to a barrio. Old brick buildings lined the street. The sidewalks held vagrants dressed in ripped or soiled clothes. Teens, dressed in pro sports team apparel, stood looking angry and leaning against buildings, the crotches of their baggy jeans hanging to their knees. Some had panty-hose caps on their heads.

"Jack, do you know what it means to be in business with me?"

There was something in Rosselli's voice that fell between tremendous intellect and the twisted meanness of a kid who ties cats to railroad tracks. He was a businessman; he was a criminal; and he had a great deal of ego and power.

"Yeah," I said.

"You think so?" Then to Chrissani: "Joey."

Chrissani turned around.

"Take a quick commission job?"

"The money right?"

"How much?"

"Five."

"Five grand it is," Frank said. "See that guy sitting alone under that broken window?"

\* \* \*

He said his name was Paul Stanley and I'll never forget watching Chrissani use a handkerchief to wipe the hand he'd used to help the man up.

They sat in front of Rosselli and myself. There was a momentary scent of dried earth, which was quickly defeated by a persistent, rank smell like feet.

"Paul Stanley," Frank said, "tell us your story."

"What kind of job do you have for me?" Paul Stanley said. "He said you had work, then you'd take me to the shelter."

Rosselli just nodded, and to this day, I don't know if Paul Stanley sensed what *I* did, if he had any idea what was coming. But he did what he was told: he talked. He had been working as a manager of a convenience store, when his wife had left. She had drained the joint account, taken his little girl, and left. He had not seen his daughter in two years. Unable to afford the mortgage, he lost his home, then his job when they found out he was living on the street.

"It's like a cycle," he said. "You don't have a job, then you're on the street, but you can't get a job if you're homeless."

Rosselli yawned. Then: "Tommy."

Giannin glanced in the rearview mirror. Rosselli jerked his head to turn. And we pulled into an alley lined with dumpsters and red brick walls.

"Hey, Frank," I said. "I get the message."

Paul Stanley had dark rings under his eyes. He glanced at Rosselli, then at me. Then he faced forward and looked out the window.

"Jack, do you know what it means to do business with me?"

The crooked grin on Rosselli's face told me that at that point, my answer didn't matter.

\* \* \*

They left the door open and Chrissani motioned the man to walk in front of him to the end of the alley. The entire thing took maybe a minute, but it seemed much longer. "Frank," I said and shook my head, pleadingly.

"I've got resources, Jack, to do just about anything."

It sounded like a loud snap.

I looked up to see Paul Stanley stiffen as if a punch had driven him upward, then pitch forward face first. The back of his head was dark with blood. Chrissani tossed his cigarette on the ground and carefully crushed it with the toe of his shoe. He lit another on the way back to the truck.

"That, Jack Austin, is what it fucking means to do business with me—life or death. Shoot 75 tomorrow and blow your sand saves and you'll get 30 percent of a million bucks."

# Chapter Twenty

———

I HAD DINNER WITH PADRE. Or tried to. Lisa had left no messages and Perkins was nowhere to be found. The restaurant was tiny and empty, but the sign out front promised "100% Authentic Mexican." It smelled of warm bread—I guessed tortillas—and Spanish rice. We ordered at the counter and an old woman handed me a number—12. Then we sat, drinking Mexican beer, waiting for our order to be called.

"You catch that number?" Padre said.

"No," I said, "but if it's 12, that's us."

He glanced at the tiny number on the table before me. Then he eyed me with a puzzled expression.

"What?" I said.

"It's 21, Jack."

"Oh, yeah, right."

"Is that dyslexia?"

"Yeah."

"Must get annoying."

"Frustrating," I said.

Padre inhaled. "They're baking tortillas."

"Yeah."

"You look distracted," he said.

I'd made it to the course late and gone directly to the range. What had I just witnessed? A guy who'd fallen on hard times and lost everything had been shot as a threat to me. Paul Stanley had been no more than a tool to Rosselli. The memory of him, seated before me, candidly speaking of how his life had fallen apart was still in my mind. The image of his corpse left in that alley, discarded like an empty bottle, was fresh, too. Rosselli had too much power and too big an ego. And I didn't want him near the Tour.

When I need to think, I hit golf balls. And I had done so afterwards—30 minutes of shanks. What could I do? Go to Chee. Sure. But what could he do? It was my word against that of Rosselli and two of his henchmen.

Even worse, now I was working for him.

"Jack." Padre lightly hit the table. "Jack."

"Sorry," I said. I had been staring out the window.

"I was asking about the money list and your status for next season?"

"I'm on the bubble."

"The dreaded 125," he said.

Padre had won twice in a four-week period last season, earning a two-year exemption.

When the food came, Padre ate like a man who'd spent the day working on his game. Likewise, I ate like a guy who'd seen a murder: I ate half a taco and stared out the window and chose the lesser of two evils to think about—my status.

There are several ways to stay on Tour. When you haven't won, but have survived for a decade, you know them all: Anyone who finishes in the top 10 one week gets into the next event; players who finish in the top 125 on the money list are exempt the following season; positions 126-150 receive partial exemption; and if you're really struggling, but have had a solid career, the Tour has exemptions for past champions and anyone who has made 150 cuts—the number to be vested in the Tour's pension plan. Of course, winning a Tour event carries a two-year exemption, and winning a Major Championship earns you as many as 10 years.

"I was checking the money list," Padre said, "and saw you're 156."

"The summer's just starting. When it gets to September, I'll worry."

"How are the wedding plans?" Padre said. He took a forkful of Spanish rice.

"You're full of good topics tonight."

"What did I say?"

"That story Lisa broke today has taken a toll."

"Want to talk about it? I'm supposed to perform the ceremony."

I sipped some beer. "The Hutch Gainer story. Lisa's been working on it for a couple months."

"Yeah?"

"It's been a huge strain on our relationship. Today she told me she wasn't sure anymore."

Padre's face held a sincere look of sorrow. He had always been a good listener. And a good friend.

"Why has it been a strain on your relationship? It's part of Lisa's job."

"I know that."

"That's a big allegation Lisa's making. A lot of players want more proof."

I pushed my plate away.

"Hutch won't confess," I said, "but the damage is done. The words 'stroke throwing' are out there."

"It's not going to help our fan base, but it won't kill us either."

"There will be doubts every time someone misses a short putt or chunks a pitch."

"Yeah," he said. We ate in silence for a while.

Then, Padre said: "I don't know if he did it or not, but he had two wins. Why throw it all away?"

I didn't say.

"You and Lisa are really are good together," Padre said. He ate another taco and looked out the window at people coming and going in the parking lot.

"Both careers demand full attention," I said.

"Makes it difficult, not impossible."

"The thing is," I said, "I like things the way they are right now."

He turned back to me. "What do you mean?"

"I don't know if we should change it. Why fix it if it's not broken?"

"You proposed."

"I know. I thought marriage would make it even better. Now I don't know."

# Chapter Twenty-One

——

ON THURSDAY, it was time to go to work, to put Hutch, Lisa, and Rosselli out of my mind. The Holiday Inn Southwest Open was to begin and I was on the range at 6:30. Perkins was next to me, wearing wraparound sunglasses, one of my Titleist hats, and a white caddie's poncho with AUSTIN on the back. Silver was still at work on his book, which was fine—Rosselli would be expecting to see Perkins on the bag anyway.

It was the first day of the tournament, and I was back—to cheat my competitors and the fans, to blow sand shots, and to shoot a 75.

"Your swing looks like shit," Perkins said.

"How do you know what a swing should look like? You're a bogey golfer."

"And you're swinging like me."

I leaned on my five-iron. "Puts what Hutch went through in a different perspective."

"Fuck Hutch. He got into it because he screwed someone out of two million. You got in this to help."

I pulled my driver and hit several mediocre tee shots. Then I grooved one. It carried the 280-yard sign and bounded out of sight. "I can't go through with it," I said.

"You don't, you'll cost Rosselli a lot of money."

"A million."

"He'll be pissed."

"I know."

* * *

It didn't take long for me to realize Rosselli didn't trust me.

On the first tee, standing behind Grant Ashley and myself, I saw Rosselli, Jenna, Gianni, and Chrissani. The gallery that follows me is not that which swarms around Tiger. So it had been easy to spot them. Players are grouped in categories and play within them to start each tournament; after the Friday cut, you play with whomever you're near on the leaderboard. Padre had won recently, so he played with the 1-A players. Next was Category 1, which consists of past winners, winners of Major Championships, and anyone in the top 25 on the all-time money list. The second tier is made up of players who have won in the last three years. Then, there was the group to which I belonged—anyone who finished in the top 125 on the money list the previous season or players with $500,000 in career earnings play together. And finally, you have Q School grads, Buy.com Tour exemptions, Monday Qualifiers, or sponsor's exemptions.

My groupies had tried to dress the part—shorts, golf shirts, and sunglasses—but looked like neither golfers nor fans. Jenna was on Rosselli's arm. Pickorino was out of the picture now and, apparently, her mourning stage had not lasted terribly long. Which made me wonder just how badly she and Rosselli wanted to be together. Enough to murder Pickorino?

I hit a decent drive and we were off. Perkins and I walked down the fairway out of earshot of the cameramen, on-course commentators, and Grant and his caddie Fur Lomax. My personal gallery followed closely.

The drive left me 155 yards to the hole. After Grant hit his approach shot, I pulled my seven-iron and stood over the ball. After 25 years of golf, I don't think about my swing unless it's off. However, with Rosselli's stare burning my back, I reviewed mental notes: swing at 80 percent; watch the clubhead meet the ball; trust yourself; stay down through impact; and follow through. I turned to look at him. He nodded and we stared at each other.

Then I took two practice swings.

I was returning from injury. No one would second-guess a 75. Except myself.

I put my approach shot in the center of the green, 15 feet from the hole. Rosselli raised his brows and moistened his lips. Then, with the rest of the small gallery, he clapped, very slowly, dropping one hand onto the other. He called out: "Start off on the right foot, Jack."

I walked to the green, where I marked my ball and examined it closely; it was new and unblemished.

"Grant, I'd like to change balls."

Grant consented. I had asked, as was the rule. A player can ask to inspect the ball for damage, but Grant was looking over his putt. I went to Perkins, rummaged through my bag—and found what I was really looking for. I slid the handheld recorder in my pocket discreetly, walked to the side of the green and, using my thumb, slowly activated the recorder.

Rosselli took off his sunglasses as I approached. "Nice shot."

Other spectators were there but hadn't gotten too close. As I had said, it was a group one would sit across the room from. But I played it safe. I had something to say that only Frank could hear. I leaned close and hugged him, like seeing a long-lost brother, and whispered: "Deal's off. I can't do it."

The craziness and evil flashed in his eyes again. But he smiled, playing along with my act, and whispered: "What the fuck are you talking about? Three hundred grand for a day's work? That's almost what the winner will make."

"And he'll earn it."

"Oh, for Christ's sake."

"Frank, I'm out."

He stopped smiling. "You listen to me. You asked to be in. You—are—in."

I shook my head and waited.

"You know," he said, "you asked a lot of very interesting questions."

"I'm careful."

"So am I. Remember the story I told you before the lobster rolls?"

I remembered it well. "No."

"Jack," Perkins said, "You're up." The Tour has five-minutes-between-shots rule. I was getting close to that limit. After a warning, you are penalized.

"Deal's off, Frank."

He leaned close to me, put a hand around my neck—and grabbed a fistful of hair. "Don't fuck with me, Austin. Seventy-five and no sand saves."

"For how much?"

"A deal is a deal. Three hundred."

I had what I needed.

He let go of me. "I'm leaving. Keep your end of this. I'll see you later."

I walked back to the green—and made birdie.

* * *

Four and a half hours later, the sun was like a flame overhead. I was three under par, and a man who killed people was angry with me. That opening-hole birdie had propelled me to a 32 on the front nine; I had needed only 12 putts. The 18th was a straight par five, 555 yards. Bunkers surrounded the front of the green with water to the left. Most players laid up and played into the green with a short iron. That was the smart play.

So I hit a three-wood off the tee and put the ball in the fairway, about 250 yards out.

Grant was one over par. "I've got to get something going," he said. "Carry me home, Jack. I've got bandages holding my swing together."

Sometimes, when you're playing with a guy who is hot, it's almost like riding his wave—you seem to play better by trying to keep up. Grant was swinging like he should have been three or four strokes over par. Instead, he was one over and still in the hunt.

As we moved down the fairway, following Grant's drive—a weak push into the left rough—Perkins said: "I'm glad you're not keeping that deal."

"I figured Jackie's got enough college money."

"The 25 grand?"

"Yeah."

"It's in an IRA in Boston for the next 18 years."

We were quiet as we walked.

"You couldn't do that, could you?" Perkins said.

"What?"

"Take dirty money."

"I did," I said.

"And it bothered you, so you gave it to me. You couldn't educate your kid with dirty money, could you?"

"At least it's going to something we both believe in: Jackie."

"But you couldn't take 300 grand for one bad round?"

"That's different."

"How?"

"Honor. I've got respect for the guys I'm competing against. And for the Tour."

"A regular Eagle Scout."

Across the fairway, Grant was surveying his lie.

"I played with Rosselli to learn information. I've got him talking about gambling on tape. And by not keeping my end of the bargain, I'm sure I'll get the opportunity to tape more."

"If he comes for you, it might not be to talk."

I forced my thoughts back to golf.

I knew my five-iron went 190 yards. I had close to 300 yards to the green, but 200 to the first bunker. The five-iron would leave me 110 to the green or 130 to the pin and it would land 10 yards short of the sand. It was the right club for a layup.

I was three under and on the first page of the leader board. I'd been beaten up and forced out of action for a month; I'd played golf with a Mafia kingpin; and now I was back and I had a chance to finish high. I'd never won. I'd come close—that sudden death playoff loss—but I had yet to win. Maybe this was my week.

Grant had tried to make up strokes, but hit a three-wood into the water.

As he stared toward the drop area, I addressed the ball, took one deep breath, and brought the five-iron back. I hit a well-positioned layup. Grant took his drop and put his fourth shot on the green. His par putt was 15 feet from the pin.

Standing over my 130-yard approach, I held an eight-iron, and choked down. I wanted to land the ball several feet short of the green and run it to the pin, so I stood closer to the ball than usual—to control the trajectory—and made an abbreviated swing. The ball flew low and finished six feet above the hole.

"Damn it," I said.

"What?" Perkins said.

"I wanted the ball beneath the hole. That's a quick putt."

Grant and I walked toward the green together. We had chatted on and off all day about soft spikes, and if they were any good. My position was that if I made a well-balanced swing, I could hit it in penny loafers. Grant said there were times when he had to really lunge at it—and make the Chi Chi Rodriguez walk-through swing—and this required the grip that only metal spikes gave. As is often the case with on-course chitchat, we never finished our discussion. At the 18th green, I saw my six-footer and went to it.

It would break sharply to the right. That was obvious as soon as I got behind the ball. Grant had honors and ran his 15-footer into the heart of the cup, to stay one over par. Then I positioned the putter's blade behind it so I would make contact off the toe of the putter, which deadened the blow—good for downhill putts. I didn't want it to run five or six feet by.

I stroked it as if the ball were an egg.

It took the line, hit the right edge of the cup and spun out, stopping two feet above the hole.

"Thing almost came all the way back," Perkins said.

I made the next putt for par and a three-under-par round of 69. I knew somewhere Frank Rosselli was furious.

\* \* \*

I was in the scorer's tent next to Grant, sipping a bottled water, thinking about my 69, and triple-checking my addition with a calculator. When you have a tendency to reverse numbers, you use a calculator.

There was some rumbling outside, then Gianni appeared and sat across from Grant and myself. Grant finished signing his card and slid it to the scorer, who seemed more concerned with doing his job than who belonged in the tent. "I thought only contestants and special passes were allowed in here," Grant said.

Gianni flashed some sort of ID. I didn't catch what it said, but knowing Rosselli, it was legit.

Grant left.

"Frank would like to see you," Gianni said to me.

I punched the numbers again. After I failed fourth-grade math, a teacher told my mother: "Face it, some kids are just slow." Thankfully, my mother did not accept that; instead, she took me from rural Maine to a specialist in Boston who diagnosed me and suggested using a calculator.

I slid the card to the scorer. "Let me see," I said, "what's tonight? Laundry is Tuesdays. I talk to my mom every Wednesday. Maybe I can squeeze him in between *Frasier* and *Seinfeld* reruns."

Gianni didn't smile.

I said: "Tell Frank I'll take him to dinner. I'd like to make it up to him. No hard feelings."

"No hard feelings?"

"Sure. I don't hold a grudge."

"*You* don't hold a grudge?"

Gianni stood and looked me over. Then he leaned close to me and whispered: "Either you've got balls the size of grapefruit or you're one dumb bastard."

"Probably the latter," I said.

# Chapter Twenty-Two

———

Jɪᴍ Dᴇᴍᴘsᴇʏ ɪɴ ᴊᴇᴀɴs, scuffed boots, a denim shirt, and a Texas-sized belt buckle—wasn't your typical sports agent, which is precisely why I hired him one night nine years ago in a Houston bar. He had played outside linebacker at Texas A&M and had a long scar on his cheek courtesy of a steer. After his football days, he had gotten a law degree and knew contracts, but our agreement was based on a handshake: he got 10 percent of any endorsement he could land me.

Dempsey, Perkins, and Chee sat in plastic chairs on the balcony of my hotel suite. My recorder lay on a square plastic table next to a six-pack of Heineken. I had changed into baggy gym shorts with the Champion emblem, a 1995 sʜᴀᴋᴇsᴘᴇᴀʀᴇ ꜰᴇsᴛɪᴠᴀʟ T-shirt, and stood barefoot, looking out past the city, at the golf course, and beyond to a distant mesa. I listened to the taped version of my conversation with Rosselli.

"'Three hundred grand for one day's work'?" Chee frowned and shook his head. "I don't know, Jack." He motioned with his chin to Dempsey. "Think that would hold up in court?"

Dempsey took a long swig of beer. "We've got him saying shoot 75 and no sand saves, but he'd have a good lawyer, too. A good lawyer could twist that around—he might've been being sarcastic or kidding. I don't know."

"Come on, you guys," I said.

"These guys have the best lawyers money can buy, Jack," Chee said. "We need all our ducks in a line before we take them on."

I leaned back against the rail and folded my arms across my chest. "Rosselli wants to meet with me."

"Alone?" Perkins said. He looked like a tourist in khaki shorts and a flowered shirt.

"I don't know," I said. "We never got to the details."

Chee stood and moved beside me. Wearing an ugly navy blue sock tie, he stared out in contemplation. It was four P.M. and the distant sun was directly across from the balcony.

Frank sent Gianni to the scorer's tent," I said. "I told him we could have dinner."

"Not good," Perkins said.

"Never get a tape recorder in there," Chee said.

"The guy lost a million bucks," Perkins said. "You're lucky he didn't take you out on the course."

"I called New Orleans PD," Chee said. "Joey is a high-priced specialist. His bodies disappear. Which explains why your homeless man is nowhere to be found."

My beer tasted flat.

"I'd expect it to be that way," Chee said. "Rosselli isn't *that* trusting. That body—and you on the stand—could put him away. Although the others in the car would no doubt counter what you said."

"Or they'd have accidents before they could testify," Perkins said.

"So what's next?" I said.

Chee and Perkins and Dempsey looked back and forth at each other.

"Great," I said. "Just great."

\* \* \*

By five-thirty, my resident legal team was still going over what-ifs? and possibilities. I knew only two things for sure: the tape provided no assurances, and I was hungry enough to eat it *and* the recorder. Rosselli hadn't contacted me about our dinner date. Lisa hadn't called, either. But a great man enjoys his own company. So I told my cohorts I was going to the hotel restaurant.

"Alone?" Perkins said. "Rosselli isn't too happy with you."

"But he hasn't contacted me."

"Could be arranging a hit."

"I've still got that .22 you gave me."

"You got a license for it?" Chee said.

"No."

He thought and said: "Take it anyway."

I nodded.

"Let me go see the DA," Chee said, "run this tape by him, see what he thinks."

"I've got a dinner meeting with some reps," Dempsey said.

"I'll eat with you, Jack," Perkins said.

"No."

"Why not?"

"I don't need a bodyguard. You don't have to baby-sit me. You're still working for Hutch Gainer. Try to find out who killed Pickorino."

"I do have some loose ends to look at," Perkins said.

"I'll meet you here after dinner," I said.

\* \* \*

When the elevator doors opened, I couldn't help but feel sorry for her. That sensation swept through me like an immediate and cold chill.

Amid golf families, she sat. In particular, I noticed her in relation to the other women—golf wives and girlfriends. Most had short haircuts; all had understated makeup and expensive jewelry.

And Jenna Andrews sat in the hotel lobby with her teased hair and a lot of mascara.

She wore a gold chain with a medallion, big gold hoop earrings, and several bracelets on each arm. Her heels were too high; her black dinner dress was too short, and cut too low. She was trying, but just didn't look the part of the conservative, stand-by-my-man golf wife. On her left leg, above the black leather strap of her high heel, she had a thin gold ankle bracelet. She held the financial section of a newspaper, but wasn't reading it. Instead she was looking around at the other women, like an insecure kid trying to fit in. And not succeeding.

I had changed into jeans, thrown loafers on my bare feet, and put on a baggy windbreaker—that hung low and conveniently housed the .22 in a pocket. Standing at the edge of the lobby, which had about 30 people in it and buzzed with conversation and activity, I watched Jenna. The usual golf crowd now included the army of journalists chasing the Hutch Gainer / John Pickorino murder story. Some golf wives waited with young kids for their husbands who probably had afternoon tee times. All the wives appeared young, even the ones I knew to be older.

I watched Jenna with empathy. Rosselli was dangerous and

mad. I didn't want to run into him. The .22 was much more useful in Perkins's hand than mine. But Rosselli and gang were not in the lobby. And through the front windows, I didn't see the black Suburban. So I took a chance and walked to Jenna. She was watching a woman putting on lipstick and never saw me coming.

"Can I talk with you for a minute?"

She looked up.

"What time are you meeting Frank?" I said.

Her eyes narrowed. "What do you want?"

"Ten minutes of your time."

"No way," she said. "I know you."

"I'd like to do this nicely, but if it comes to it, we both know I know all about you two-timing Pickorino. And we both know the cops would find that very interesting."

"I talked to them. A guy asked me all about it. I got nothing to say to you."

"Ten minutes," I said.

"I'm waiting for someone. Beat it."

"Frank?"

"None of your goddamned business." She didn't look like the insecure, lonely woman of the previous minute. Now she was tough. I guessed she had learned how to act tough. Gianni had said she'd been a stripper in Houston. There were few professions more degrading. That in itself would have bred toughness.

"If not Frank, who?"

"Scram."

She was nervous, shifting in her seat.

"You look embarrassed to be seen with me." I knew it might be the other way around—maybe she didn't want me to see who she was waiting for. "Maybe I can tag along with you and your friend," I said. "How about the three of us grab something to eat?"

She stood up and left the lobby.

\* \* \*

She didn't wait for the elevator; she took the stairs. There was something going on. If she were dining with Rosselli, why not wait and have him deal with me? Had she heard he was mad at Dear Old Jack and, thus, didn't want to be seen with me? As I followed her, I knew she was afraid. I remembered her bruised hand and thought fear was a reasonable response; her taste in men was less than stellar.

The stairwell was cement and her heels clacked as she climbed. I removed my loafers and followed at a discreet distance.

She went to the fourth floor. In heels, the fourth floor was a long walk. She really wanted to get away from me. She was thin and her alibi suggested she worked out. Her figure belied her age, which had to be mid-to-late thirties.

In the hallway of the fourth floor, I put the loafers on and closed the distance between us, coming up on her side. "Here's Johnny."

She stopped short. "What the fuck are you doing?"

"Nice mouth."

"Go to hell."

"Ten minutes."

She stood staring, considering, and, like a good salesman, I rushed forward. "What can ten minutes do?"

"I don't even know you. You could be some weirdo."

"Given your male companions, how bad can I be?"

"Johnny was a nice old man."

"A real gem," I said. "Ten minutes."

She started to speak, but I said: "Ten minutes and you'll never see me again."

"He'll come looking for me when I'm late."

"Then we'll go to my room."

* * *

My room was three more flights. She was moving slowly. I would be, too, after seven flights of stairs in high heels.

"Tough walking in those?"

"Not bad."

"Take them off."

She shook her head. "It's O.K. Besides, he likes it when I wear them."

"Frank?"

"Don't play games, Mister."

"Call me Jack. Here—" I leaned toward her and scooped her up, one arm behind her back, the other beneath her legs.

"What are you doing?"

"I interrupted your dinner plans. I won't make you walk eight flights in heels, too."

As we climbed, her eyes narrowed and examined my face. I guessed no one had ever tried to save her a long walk before. Her back was taut beneath my arm as if she were tense. Her legs were thin and muscular, dancer's legs.

I set her down, careful not to have the short skirt rise.

"You didn't have to do that."

"I know."

"You're strong."

I grinned and couldn't resist: "Never had a cavity, either."

\* \* \*

Perkins was not in my room. For that matter, neither was Lisa.

Jenna waited for me to ask her in, then sat in the chair next to the round corner table. I sat on the loveseat.

"I don't have much," I said, "only beer."

"No thanks. What do you want?"

"How's life without John Pickorino?"

"Why do you ask?"

"You miss him?"

"Sure."

"How's your hand?"

"What do you mean?"

"You know what I mean."

"No, I don't." She leaned back in the chair and glanced around the room. "That suitcase looks expensive. You travel light."

"A lot of practice. You're not a good liar."

"I don't need your shit, preppy."

"The loafers always give me away. How was it living with Pickorino? He almost broke your hand."

"He did break it. But it was better than the alternative." She had a cold, hard stare.

"What the hell was your alternative?"

Her eyes were blue and very big as she leaned forward. "Five years ago I was in Houston dancing—stripping."

I knew most of that already.

"He came to the club one night and I tabled for him. He tipped me a hundred bucks. He came the next night and I left with him. I've been with him ever since."

"But not anymore."

"No. Not anymore."

"So that was it. You left with him and never went back?"

"Would you?"

"I don't know. When did the abuse begin?"

"You have a cigarette?"

"Sorry."

"Then I'll have that beer," she said.

I got up to get her one. As I moved to the fridge, I found myself feeling for her. Pickorino had treated her poorly. Could Frank be a step up? I shut the fridge behind me and brought her the beer. She drank from the bottle.

"You never answered my question," I said.

"What?"

"The abuse?"

"Couple months into it. I didn't want to do something—" she gave a small flutter with her hand "—sexual. So he hit me."

"And?"

"And what?"

"And you didn't leave?"

"You ever stripped?" She set the bottle on the chair and leaned forward again. Her dress was low-cut. "Do you know what I am?"

We were quiet for a long time.

I said: "An intelligent woman."

"Bullshit." She looked away.

"You're smart enough to know your situation. Many people aren't. Leave Frank."

Her eyes began to moisten. "You know what strippers do when they get old, when someone young and cute bounces in who doesn't know the way things really are? You know what happens to them when they get replaced?"

Very softly, I said: "No."

She was crying now. "They become whores. Strippers never make it. I used to think they could. I listened to the others talk in the dressing room when I was young. 'I'm only here for a year.' Or 'I'll leave after a month.' No one left. They got old. They got replaced. My friends whored and some got AIDS. Some OD'ed. John Pickorino was my way out."

"I understand."

"So I can stand a slap every now and then."

She was using the present tense.

"When did you get with Frank?"

"I met him at a hotel a few months back. John took me to a gambling thing."

"Gambling?"

"In a hotel room. He didn't say much, but they talked about golf and—"

"What were they saying?"

"Huh? I don't know. But Frank was nice."

"What were they doing?"

She shook her head. "I don't know. John didn't explain it. I talked to Frank."

She didn't know anything about golf or the operation. So I said: "And now Pickorino's gone. Just you and Frank."

"What's that mean?"

"Frank's nice and now Pickorino's gone. Convenient."

"I don't need that. I didn't kill anyone." She stood.

"No," I said, "I'm sure Frank took care of that and made it look like Hutch Gainer did it."

"You don't know what you're talking about."

"Do you?"

She wouldn't look at me as she walked out.

# Chapter Twenty-Three

―――

I SAT ON THE BALCONY waiting for room service to deliver three tuna sandwiches and drank a leftover Heineken as I thought. It was dark; evening was fast becoming night and growing cold. The golf course below was still and silent. Lisa hadn't spoken to me since saying she'd be happier without me around; a man I believed to be innocent of murder was sitting in a jail cell; and I still didn't know who killed John Pickorino.

Jenna Andrews had a motive. Rosselli, as difficult as it was to believe, seemed a step up for her—maybe not a leap, but compared to a man who had broken her hand, he had to be an improvement. That spoke to motive in terms of her emotional well-being. Who got Pickorino's money? She had been with him five years. Was she in his will? Was she his common-law wife? That would give her his estate. Five years in an abusive relationship was a long time. She probably deserved Pickorino's money. Five years? A long time. It made me wonder what her childhood had been like. How had she ended up stripping? And what would come after Rosselli? Yet no matter how much empathy I felt, Hutch Gainer was still in jail for a crime he didn't commit.

Money often leads to murder. And Pickorino's death had left a lot for someone. Jenna had broken down and cried in front of me. Could she have shot a man point-blank? She was tough but I didn't think in that way.

Inside, I sat on the loveseat, finished my last sandwich and, on my laptop, searched for information regarding common-law

―――

marriages. A site entitled Legal Information Network stated they
had begun during frontier times and listed states that currently
had laws regarding them. Texas was one. Residents of Texas seek-
ing a common-law marriage had only to go to their county clerk
and sign a form. Had Jenna and Pickorino signed one? They were
husband and wife if they had. That would probably entitle Jenna to
Pickorino's money. But wouldn't Pickorino have originally introduced Jenna as his wife if they were married? I tried to remember
how he had introduced her. Had he introduced her at all?
Dempsey could find out who was handling the estate and if they
had filed for common-law marriage.

* * *

When the knock came, I had been on the bed, groggily reading
*King Lear*. I sprung to my feet and rifled through the dresser door
for the .22. Frank—or rather Chrissani—had finally come. There
was no telling where Perkins was. So, frantically, I dug Chee's
number out of my wallet.

I had the number nearly dialed when I heard Lisa's voice.

She looked beautiful in khaki shorts, a thin, long-sleeved dark
sweater, and tan flats. When I opened the door, her eyes fell to the gun.

"It's been that kind of day," I said.

"What's going on?"

"Come in. I'll tell you."

She stepped inside and froze. "It smells like perfume."

"Jenna Andrews was here."

"Who?"

"Pickorino's girlfriend—who is currently seeing Frank Rosselli
and had been two-timing Pickorino."

"What are you talking about?"

"Long story. What's new with Hutch?"

She came in and sat on the loveseat. "God, that fragrance is
strong."

"Yeah." I sat beside her.

"The room service tray—did you have dinner with her?"

"I'm engaged."

"Answer the question."

"No, Lisa, I love you."

"I love you, too."

"Jenna had been with Pickorino for five years."

"The woman from the hospital room?"

"Yeah. I thought she might know something."

"Does she?"

"Probably."

"She's not telling?"

No," I said. "She's had a tough life. Her looks are all she has. And they're not enough."

"What's that mean?"

"She was a stripper in Houston when she got hooked up with Pickorino. An abusive relationship."

"That's awful—but she made a choice to stay with him."

"Maybe."

"People have choices, Jack."

"Easy to say that for you and me. She started from ground zero."

"You started in remedial classes and earned a college degree. People control their destinies."

"I had parents who gave a damn. Makes a difference."

Lisa sighed. "You're taking in another stray."

I didn't say anything.

"It's one of the things I love about you, your compassion. But you can't save everyone."

I got up and turned off the light. A lamp inside the bedroom splashed onto the carpet. Lisa's expression was tranquil; her hands rested quietly in her lap. I sat down next to her again.

"The breeze coming from the balcony feels nice," she said.

"The dark is calming," I said.

"Have you learned anything?" she said.

"Not much. Still believe Hutch did it?"

"The evidence still points to him, Jack."

"He's innocent."

She leaned back and exhaled. She said: "He threw strokes."

I saw the way her hair hung at an angle across her shoulder.

"You're not denying that?" she said.

"I watched a homeless man get shot," I said. "They left him on the side of a dirt road. I was offered 300 grand to shoot 75 today."

She got up and the lights went on with a click. "What are you telling me, Jack?"

"We haven't really talked in days. Enough is enough."

She went to the chair near the table.

"We haven't been the same since I got involved with Hutch," I said. "The situation is getting out of hand."

"Jack."

"I cost Frank a million bucks today. I've gotten in the middle of something dangerous."

She inhaled slowly and I could see her thinking. She started to say something, then closed her mouth. "Why?" she said. "No, I *know* why. To keep the cheating from going public."

"Yes."

"For that, tell me why?"

"The game."

"Even if it means your life?"

"No." I got off the loveseat and leaned against the wall, my arms folded across my chest.

"So, Hutch did it?"

"I'm trusting you," I said.

"I know."

At the door, we kissed. It wasn't a peck on the cheek. It was the type of kiss that leads to more. But it didn't on this night. Not while Frank was angry and I needed a .22 next to my argyle socks.

\* \* \*

Friday morning at six, I woke and stared at the cot where Perkins had been sleeping. It was still folded, crisp white sheets and green wool blanket creased neatly. I called the desk. He hadn't tried to call. I called the Albuquerque Police Station to speak to Chee. He wasn't in. Perkins knew when my tee time was; if he didn't show for that, then it was time to worry.

\* \* \*

I was in the bustling locker room by 7:00 A.M. even though I wasn't slated to go off until 1:22 P.M. Some players were in golf attire and others had on workout clothes similar to the loose windbreaker and gray sweatpants I wore. Some read papers; others watched the news; still others spoke on phones set up on a corner table, courtesy of AT&T. At the Holiday Inn Southwest Open, my Thursday-Friday tee times were morning-afternoon; Saturday and Sunday tee times are dictated by score—first place plays last; last plays first.

Sandwiches for dinner had left me hungry so I sat in front of my locker with a full plate: omelet, spicy hash browns, and toast. I drank coffee and orange juice. The locker was beautiful oak; the design on the door looked handcrafted. You take note of things like that when your father is a carpenter. My name, in black lettering, was on a nameplate. Inside were new Footjoy gloves; two-week-old Dryjoy shoes; and four dozen Titleist balls. The Tour is the good life, every kid's dream. I tried not to lose sight of that and after talking to Kiko and Jenna, it was easy to keep things in perspective.

However, there was something unexpected in my locker as well: a hand-scribbled note taped to the inside of the door.

# Chapter Twenty-Four

———

How had Ron Giacomin gotten in the locker room? His note requested a meeting with me. Why? He hadn't even stuck around after we beat him and the Phillips kid from the Buy.com Tour. Rosselli was using Giacomin's bookie, that much I knew. Had Giacomin gotten wind of my original arrangement with my "partner"? What else could it be?

But Frank Rosselli was careful. He had said his stroke-throwing scheme was a business venture. If he were the one behind Hutch Gainer's blackmail requests, then he had a business venture already in place. Given Frank's suggested scheme featuring Moi, it didn't make sense for him to be the one blackmailing Hutch. Wouldn't two be risky? But that was how I thought. Would he think the same way? In any case, someone in the gambling ring that Jenna had described had indeed blackmailed Hutch. And entering that ring was the only way to find out who.

I placed my plate atop the stack of dirty ones and went to the AT&T table. Tour players are allowed free phone calls worldwide during events. I dialed information, and asked for the number to the capitol in Austin, Texas. I got it and began looking into the possible common-law marriage of the late John Pickorino and Jenna Andrews.

A half-hour later, I had my answer: "Johnny Pick" and Jenna were not husband and wife. So who was getting all that money? Made me wish I'd been nicer to Pickorino.

* * *

I was heading to the fitness van when Giacomin called my name. He was alone and looked the same as he had on the golf course—long blonde hair, tall and thin, and dressed in designer wear from sunglasses to sneakers.

I led Giacomin into the clubhouse, where I showed my Tour ID—my money clip—to the maitre d'. The ID allows players and guests into the dining facilities at Tour events for meals at no charge. Giacomin and I sat at a small table with a white linen tablecloth, china, and silver flatware. Between us a single rose stemmed from a tiny vase. No one else was around.

A waitress offered us menus. She was tall and thin and maybe 25 with long brown hair and dark eyes. She wore a skirt. I felt guilty for noticing; when Lisa was around I never looked.

I asked for coffee.

Giacomin opened his menu, looked it over, then gave up. "What's good?"

"Oh, everything, sir."

"Scrambled eggs, toast, coffee."

"How many eggs, sir?"

"Jesus, I don't care. Two."

"Very good, sir." She left.

"How well do you know Frank Rosselli, Jack?"

"I played that one time with him. That's it."

The waitress filled my cup and left.

"I've got some very important information for you."

I sipped my coffee, my eyes locked on his.

"It's stuff you'd be *really* interested in."

The dining room was majestic and the coffee lived up to expectations. "What is it, Giacomin?"

He shook his head.

"No?"

"Uh-huh."

"Why?"

"I want something in return."

"What a surprise."

The waitress returned with Giacomin's breakfast.

"Fast service," I said and smiled at her. When she was gone I said: "Here's your trade: I'll buy you breakfast."

"I don't think so." Giacomin used his knife and fork to eat his eggs, meticulously wiping his thin face after each bite. "I'm a businessman. When I hear something I can sell, I do it."

"How much?"

"Virtually free," he said and smiled like he was talking a 17-year-old into a car with two hundred thousand miles on it. "What do you know about Rosselli's gambling?"

"Not a thing."

"Nothing?"

"Nada."

"Well, he gambles big money on golf."

I smiled. "Let me guess, and you do as well."

He bit into a piece of toast that was cut into a triangle. "Correct. Rosselli has lost a great deal of money to me recently."

"To you?"

"Yeah. I just said that."

I said: "He usually lose?"

Giacomin eyes went from his food to mine. He chewed slowly. "Recently, he's lost. Last season he made a killing, though."

But not this season, which made the possibility of Rosselli blackmailing Hutch seem even more remote—but offered up Giacomin as a suspect.

"What would you be willing to do in exchange for information which could save your life, Jack?"

Two players dressed for their tee times walked into the room. They waved. I returned the gesture. Giacomin stared down at his plate. The players sat down across the room.

"What's your deal?"

"I'd like to bet on your score today."

"Against Frank?"

"You don't need to know that."

"You want me to shoot a particular score for information. What's the information?"

"Will you do it?"

"What's the information about?"

He shook his head.

"How much detail can you provide?"

"A lot."

I simply nodded.

"Rosselli has a hit-man in town to take you out tomorrow night."

I sipped my coffee and looked at Giacomin. "How do you know that?"

"I talk to people."

"I want the source," I said. "How can I trust that?"

"You can trust it because I'm goddamned well connected. Shoot a 74 or higher. You want a description of the guy?"

I shook my head. I'd know Chrissani.

"No?"

"No," I said. "I shot 69 yesterday. I'm tied for fifth place."

"What's that mean?"

"Means I'd be a fool to throw strokes."

"We have a deal."

"You said details—when, where, why, how?"

"It's going down in the hotel."

"Shoot me in the hotel?"

"You don't believe me?"

I lied to him: "I think you're full of shit."

"We've got a deal."

I stood and moved around the table. Hutch was in jail; Pickorino was dead; and my relationship with Lisa was strained. All because of a group of men betting on my colleagues and me like dogfights. My face was getting hot, my jaws clenched. I grabbed his jacket and lifted him out of his chair. It went over backward.

"No deal," I said and tossed him down in a heap. No one waved as I walked out.

* * *

On the putting green, I was dressed for golf, but my mind was far from my putting stroke. I saw Perkins strolling toward me. He was dressed for work: poncho, shorts, running shoes, and aviator sunglasses. It was 11:00 A.M.

"Jesus Christ," Perkins said, "that missed by two feet."

"You know, some players think of their caddies as sports psychiatrists."

"I'm not a caddie."

"Where were you last night?"

"Watching Kiko's room. You'll never guess who showed up there at 2:00 A.M. and left early this morning."

"Who?"

"Jenna."

He broke my stare by throwing the three balls back to me. "Putt," he said. "You need the practice."

* * *

By 1:15, I stood near the tee and watched the group preceding us hit. The sweet smell of desert scrub brush was in the air, like pine and eucalyptus. Grant Ashley and I were paired again. We shared small talk, but it wasn't genuine; each of us was thinking, although I assumed he had his mind on golf. I had told Perkins what I'd learned from Giacomin. He didn't seem too concerned, but never did. And it wasn't him that Rosselli was after.

The best professional tournament I'd ever played had been when I'd had the flu. I was so sick, I didn't think about golf. My first drive was similar to that experience. The ball carried 300 yards and rolled nearly 30 more into the heart of the fairway. The first hole was what I considered a birdie hole—par four, 400 yards, and today there was no wind, almost unheard of for early spring in the desert.

"Got your head back on golf," Perkins said.

"Somewhat."

"Jesus," Grant said, on his way to the tee, "had your Wheaties today." He took three practice swings, then hit driver 275 yards down the middle.

\* \* \*

As Perkins and I moved down the fairway, someone called my name.

Dempsey waved me over to the rope separating the gallery from the fairway. We walked on opposite sides of the rope.

"Had dinner with people representing a new golf ball," Dempsey said.

"Gaalf baals," I said.

"This is serious. How would you feel about switching?"

"From Titleist? No way."

"Jack, you haven't even hit these new balls. Titleist gives the big money to—guys who've won Majors."

"And I'll win one very soon."

"Listen, these guys are looking for a long hitter and are talking six figures, plus incentives and bonuses."

"Tell them to chase the long-drive contestants. I'm a golfer not an axe swinger. I appreciate the effort, Jim. But I've played the same ball since I was 19. I've won some big tournaments with it."

"You've never won on Tour."

I stopped walking. "Before the Tour," I said. "And I'm close."

"It's a lot of money."

"It's not about money."

We paused to watch Grant hit. It looked like a hard wedge and he flew the green. Perkins was waiting at my ball.

"I've got one more thing," I said to Dempsey. "Can you find out who gets Pickorino's money?"

"Probably. And Chee said the DA needs more than just that tape."

"Figures," I said and went to Perkins.

The drive had left me 75 yards to the front edge, 90 to the hole. In actuality, my drive hadn't been a smart play. I tried to always leave myself a full swing. I knew my nine-iron carried 130 yards, my pitching wedge traveled 120, and my 60-degree wedge topped-out at 100. This would be an abbreviated 60-degree.

I took two practice swings, then moved to the ball.

And executed. It landed maybe six feet behind the cup, then spun back, and stopped inches from the hole.

"Nice action on that," Grant said.

And my agent wanted me to change balls.

* * *

On the green, Grant looked at my ball and shook his head. "Big advantage to being long off the tee. That's a kick-in."

He missed his birdie chip by inches and tapped in for par. He was still one stroke over par, having shot a 73 Thursday. I guessed the cut would be one under, maybe two. If he wanted security, he needed to make birdies.

I tapped in my six-inch birdie, moving me to five-under. I made another birdie on the front nine and went out in 34, totaling five-under for the tourney.

* * *

After four consecutive pars, I stood on the tee of the 14th, a dogleg, 585-yard par five and looked out over the hole. The fairway was very narrow, the rough thick and high. This was a risk-reward hole. Our gallery was a little larger than Thursday's. It was Friday and maybe a few golf nuts had called in sick. Many of the people were waiting to see what Grant and I would attempt. I didn't need my calculator to tell me that even if I hit a 300-yard drive, that would still leave 285 to the green. I would have to hit driver-driver to reach it in two.

Perkins handed me the three-wood.

"Driver," I said.

"Yesterday you put your second shot in the woods."

"But I saved par." I reached past him and pulled the driver, took the head cover off, and tossed it to him. I teed the ball high; I wanted to keep it in the air as long as I could to get maximum distance.

I hit a long straight drive.

"You look like Daly today," Grant said. He hit a three-wood safely into the fairway, well behind my ball. Then he hit his second to within a hundred yards of the green.

At my ball, Perkins and I looked my second shot over. The sun was above the green like a yellow wafer on the horizon. I had a straight shot at the pin, but the wind had picked up slightly and the air smelled of dust; when I ran a hand through my hair it felt like straw.

As I stood behind the ball and prepared to hit my driver off the fairway, I glanced around. The gallery had dispersed and now there were only a handful of spectators. A father had gotten his son out of school for the day. When I made eye contact with them, the boy waved. I smiled and waved back. Dempsey was 10 feet from them. He gave me thumbs up. Behind him, a man I thought I recognized but momentarily couldn't place, stood wearing navy blue shorts, white athletic socks pulled to mid-calf, tennis shoes, and a bright red and yellow golf shirt; he had on dark glasses. Detective Mike Chee's legs made my golf ball look tanned. He made no gesture when I spotted him.

To Perkins I said: "See the guy behind Dempsey."

"Sure. Chee's been there since the first hole."

"Yeah?"

"I'm a trained private investigator, Jack."

"What's he doing here?"

"You don't notice a hell of a lot do you?"

"I'm working."

"Look to Chee's right, about three people deep."

Giacomin stood beside Kiko.

"Figured the game is tough enough without telling you you're being followed and the guys following you are being followed as well," Perkins said.

I took maybe five practice swings to get my head together. I was being followed. It hadn't taken Kiko long to update his resume and find a new gig. I felt like going to Giacomin and throwing him around again. But how would that look to the kid who'd waved?

No good for the game. Of course, everything else I'd tried to do with the game in mind since I'd met Hutch had failed. I didn't make a scene. Besides, I had a bodyguard. And a cop was watching their every move.

My next swing produced a low, line-drive duck-hook that landed in the left rough.

# Chapter Twenty-Five

——

PERKINS, CHEE, AND I were sitting in my hotel suite again. My mind was on the final holes. I had begun the day in fifth place, but had blown three strokes on the last five holes to finish with a 73, leaving me — 69, 73 — totaling two under par and tied for 18th.

The phone rang.

Lisa said: "Want to get dinner?"

"I'm being followed."

"You O.K.?"

"Of course."

"I miss you."

"Me, too," I said. "I miss you more than you know."

Perkins was sitting at the corner table. "How sweet."

"Tell him to shut up."

I told Perkins to shut up. He grinned. Chee sat in the desk chair.

"Who is following you, Jack?"

"Rosselli. But there might be second guy now."

"You don't know for sure?"

"No."

"Jesus," she said.

We were quiet for a moment.

"What can I do?" she said.

"Nothing."

"I love you."

"I love you, too."

"And, Jack—"

——

"Yeah?"

"Don't try that second shot on 14 tomorrow."

"I love it when you talk golf."

She laughed and hung up. It was good to hear her laugh; it had been too long since I'd heard it.

I picked up the phone again, dialed room service, and ordered a steak—well done, baked potato, a salad, ranch dressing, and bottled water. Perkins was drinking beer; Chee had brought his own coffee.

"Last night," Chee said, "I was following Jenna Andrews and she led me to Kiko's room, where I found your buddy here."

"So you followed Kiko and he led you to Giacomin?" I said.

"Yeah. And to the golf course, where I found you."

"Things make even less sense," I said. "I should've ordered something much stronger than water."

"Is Jenna involved with Kiko?" Perkins said.

"If you consider spending the night being involved with him," Chee said.

"So both Rosselli and Kiko have the same motive to murder Pickorino," I said. "Jenna Andrews, the deceased's girlfriend."

"I never liked Kiko's alibi—dinner with his aunt. She's blind and deaf, but she goes along with his time frame."

"And Jenna went in late last night and came out this morning," I said.

"Yeah," Perkins said.

"And Kiko had access to both Hutch and Pickorino," I said.

"But his prints were where they should be," Chee said. "And that goddamned alibi is very good."

"Innocent murder suspects hardly ever have good alibis," Perkins said.

"I had a long talk with Jenna last night," I said.

Chee looked at me over his paper cup.

"What?" Perkins said.

I told them about it.

"So you feel bad for her?" Chee said.

"To some degree."

"Even if she's a murderer?" Perkins said.

"I don't think she is."

"Anyone can do it," Perkins said, "and most will for the right reasons."

Someone knocked on the door; the peephole showed room service.

"Could you make out what Kiko and Giacomin were talking about on the course?" I said to Chee, after room service had left the food.

"They weren't speaking."

"That's odd," I said. "Intimidation?"

"Possibly."

I told them about my meeting with Giacomin that morning. Perkins had heard it all during my final holes, on the golf course, but listened intently again.

"So the question is," I said, "why is Kiko with Giacomin? Is he so pissed that he can't wait for Chrissani to do it?"

"It's nice to be so popular," Chee said.

"Could be a race," Perkins said. "There's a lot of could-be's, ifs, and maybes in all this."

* * *

Later, Dempsey arrived, grinning ear to ear. "I got your information and yaw'll love this." His eyes ran to the beers. "Have one?"

Perkins got one and handed it to Dempsey.

"Mr. John Pickorino—being the kind old gentleman he was—left his estate to charity."

"It's dirty," Chee said.

"That's the kicker," Dempsey said. "It's completely legit. He never had a will and two weeks ago drew one up and left almost half his money to an orphanage and the rest—in ten-grand donations—to hundreds of charities. From AIDS research to the Catholic Church."

I was getting a migraine and had barely touched my steak. Jenna and Kiko? Pickorino a philanthropist? But he had mentioned making good and being orphaned.

"He mentioned doing something like that," I said. "He said it was his way of making good for the things he'd done in his life."

"Typical," Chee said. "Guy like that thinks he can buy everything, even forgiveness."

"How long are they going to hold Hutch?" I said to Chee.

"Depends," Chee said, "in court, stroke-throwing, blackmail and fingerprints would hold up better than a love triangle. Besides, whoever did it thinks they got away with it."

"Nice system."

"It's how things work, Jack," Perkins said.

\* \* \*

Above the city, the sky was a lake of ink. I had eaten an early dinner. It was too late to risk getting lost in Albuquerque, so I took a cab.

At the address I'd requested, I tipped well and asked the cab-driver—who did not speak—to wait. I didn't know how long I'd be and there was no mistaking the neighborhood: I was in the barrio. There was no driveway; an open dirt yard led to the faded adobe house that was no larger than a one-car garage and windowless from my vantage point. None of the homes in this neighborhood had lawns—the cost of grass, or rather water to grow it, made lawns symbols of status in desert regions. Young kids played in the street, which was lit by one street-lamp; the others had been broken. Some kids had bare feet and all wore soiled clothing. There was the rapid, rhythmic hum of Spanish. As I neared the front door, I smelled cooking—baking bread and spices.

I knocked three times. When the door finally opened, Kiko's alibi stood before me.

She was tiny and frail, up to my chest, with a thin neck, and a face the color of almonds and wrinkled, like skin too long in water. Her frost-colored hair made her hue appear darker. She wore a large hearing aid and pop-bottle glasses.

She opened the door.

"Mi llamo es Jack."

She said nothing, only tilted her head and looked up at me.

"I see my Spanish has improved."

"I speak Spanish," she said. "Those people"—she looked over my shoulder—"speak Spanglish. They butcher the language."

"I'm Jack Austin, Mrs..."

"Soccorro. Luz Soccorro." She pronounced her last name rolling the r's authentically.

"I'd appreciate it if you could spare a few minutes of your time."

"For what?"

"To talk about your nephew, Kiko."

"Is he O.K.?"

"He's fine."

"What then?"

She looked like a quiet little old lady, but there was more to her. She was sharp and careful.

The open door offered light and more of the aroma from within; something smelled Cajun. The noise from the street had died down, as children went home. My guess was nighttime in this neighborhood spawned activity not fit for children or a 90-year-old woman. Or a 35-year-old golfer.

I wondered how long the cabby would wait.

"May I come in?"

She held the door and we entered the kitchen. It was the main room. Directly beyond it was a short hall with two doors. The floor was red tile. There was sand on it. This time of year, with the wind, you would need a very well-constructed home to keep the sand out. On the kitchen table, there was a carefully centered dinner plate with mismatched silverware and a plastic cup filled with water. She had set the table, despite cooking for one. There was a certain amount of pride in that, which spoke volumes. There were two chairs, one was old and made of wood; the other was a metal folding chair. Both were scarred. Next to the wooden one was a large bag with what looked like an afghan in it with a huge needle protruding.

She went to the stove. Grease streaked the pan like gasoline in rainwater. She was cooking tortillas in oil and rolling meat and chiles and cheese in them. Enchiladas.

"Please sit."

I went to the metal chair.

She turned off the stove, fixed two plates, and brought me one. Then she got me silverware and a glass of water from the tap.

"I'm interrupting," I said. "You eat, I just wanted to ask—"

She set my water in front of me, then moved around the table, and sat. "At my age, any company is welcomed. You're too thin for your height. Eat."

"Thank you." I cut the enchiladas and took a bite. Sweat formed almost instantaneously on my forehead. I gulped water.

It made her smile.

"When was the last time you saw Kiko?" I said.

For her, the enchiladas seemed to go down like warm milk. I was a *gringo*.

"Tuesday." She took off her glasses and set them next to her as she ate.

I took a second bite, trying to keep things casual. "When did he arrive and leave?"

"Five to eight."

It sounded rehearsed.

"And you're sure of that?"

"Yes."

I finished my enchiladas and wiped my forehead on my sleeve, letting some time pass, an attempt to set her at ease.

"Was that clock here when Kiko arrived?"

She squinted hard toward the wall over the stove. The clock was large and round like the ones in classrooms. "Yes. Why are you asking? I told the police already."

"I know. And I appreciate your time."

"You're a police officer?"

I drank some water. I don't know if she thought I affirmed that, but she sighed.

"So I'll answer the questions again. And what will you do for me when those kids break in again? I'm an old lady. They steal my things. Last year one of them knocked me down."

"Did you call the local authorities?"

"They didn't help."

"Can you tell me everything that happened Tuesday night?"

"Kiko came over for dinner. It was nice. I hadn't seen him in years."

Convenient time to pop in. "Were you with him the entire time he was here?"

"Yes."

She stood and cleared the table. At the sink, she turned on the water and held up a dish to examine it. "Can you bring my glasses?"

I got them and went to her. "You sit, Mrs. Soccorro. I'll do them."

"No, no." I nodded and she went to the table. I didn't feel good about leading her on—she had trusted me and fed me. But Chee didn't buy Kiko's alibi. And her answers seemed stiff, forced.

I washed and spoke over my shoulder: "What did you and Kiko talk about?"

"His mother. I told him how proud she'd be of him. He's got a very good job, you know, running that business in New Orleans."

"Of course. So, were you with him the entire time he was here?"

"What?"

She was knitting. I repeated the question and glanced back at her.

"I went to use the restroom, maybe." She yawned.

Being in this neighborhood, chatting with an old woman who street punks took advantage of brought back Kiko's comment about my seemingly having it all. I had talked about his life—and seen how that was—met Jenna Andrews, who would give up physical well-being to avoid what life had offered her; and I had listened to Paul Stanley tell of his losses. As I stood doing the dishes, I didn't feel good about much of anything. I had a life any of them would die to have. And now I stood in Luz Soccorro's impoverished kitchen trying to catch her in a lie.

"Must've been good to catch up," I said over my shoulder.

No answer.

I looked behind me. She was asleep in her chair. The clock said 7:10. I didn't enjoy it, but I had what I had come for. I finished the dishes and locked the door behind me.

\* \* \*

Kiko opened his hotel room door an inch; it was chained.

"You don't look happy to see me," I said.

He had taken off the satin jacket, but still wore black jeans and cowboy boots. He had on an ironed white T-shirt. His ponytail pulled his hair tight.

"Beat it," he said.

"How come you talk like a fifties movie? 'Beat it,' and 'Bub.'"

"You're not a real popular guy."

"That's what I hear."

"I'd stay in your room, if I were you."

"Can I come in?"

"You hear what I said?"

"Yeah."

"I don't know if you're stupid or brave," he said.

"Learning disabled people have higher-than-average IQs," I said.

"What?"

"Open up."

We stood like that for a while, then he shook his head. Maybe he was curious as to what I might say; regardless, he opened the door. I sat on the edge of the bed. He moved past me and leaned against the dresser. The TV was on and race cars were going around in circles.

"I never took you for a golf fan," I said. "But I saw you today. Glad to know you are."

He shifted his weight and crossed his arms.

"You with Giacomin now?" I asked.

"None of your business."

"Well, you're still here. Either that's to be with Jenna or you've found work."

"It's none of your business. And I don't like you showing up here, running your mouth."

"Just looking out for your career. Going from Pickorino to Giacomin is a step down."

"Think you know it all, don't you?" He smiled at how dumb I was.

"I do know a lot of things."

"You got no idea, Pal."

"Pal." I shook my head. "There you go again."

He said nothing.

"I know someone's in town to hit me."

"Really?" He lifted himself up and sat atop the dresser. "And how do you know that?"

"You know the answer."

"No. But I am curious."

His face was contemplative. I didn't think he was lying. That would mean he had not spoken to Giacomin about our breakfast meeting—which made me doubt he was with Giacomin full time.

"Giacomin hire you to just stand there and try to intimidate me?"

"Try to? You hit into the woods."

"That's just my normal ball flight." I grinned.

He exhaled and leaned forward. "It was an easy grand."

"From Giacomin?"

"You think I'm a thug, don't you?"

"I know you want to cook, to run a restaurant."

"That costs money. Today I made a grand."

"To stand there?"

"Yeah. I'm not some billionaire golfer."

"Neither am I," I said.

"You've got more money than I'll see in a lifetime."

"Maybe," I said.

There was six-pack of Budweiser cans on the windowsill. He went to it, got one, pulled the tab, and drank. He didn't offer me one.

"Giacomin is a twerp," he said. "When Johnny was around, I had a run-in with Giacomin. Asshole treated me like a waiter, telling me to get him drinks."

"I saw Pickorino do that to you."

"But Pickorino was paying me."

"Did he know you were sleeping with his girlfriend?"

The can stopped inches from his lips. He stared at me over the can, then slowly lowered it.

"A guy saw her walk in here last night and leave this morning," I said.

He shook his head again. "You got a fucking mouth on you, Austin." He took in some beer, held it before swallowing like a man taste-testing fine wine. Except he stood staring at me.

"She's a nice woman," I said. "I hope you treat her better than

Pickorino did."

"I do."

"Must've pissed you off to see the way Pickorino treated her."

"Nice try." He smiled. "You got the wrong cat."

"There you go with the fifties again."

"I didn't do it." He was cool. And why not? He had his alibi. But that alibi had fallen asleep an hour earlier than he had supposedly left her home the night Pickorino was shot.

"You had a lot to gain with Jenna," I said.

"I don't need anymore jive," he said.

"And if no one proves you did it, you'll get all the money."

He tried to play it cool and glanced slowly at his beer can. "What money?"

I laughed. "You haven't seen the will?"

"He didn't have a will."

I leaned back, tilted my head, and stared at him. "You're serious, aren't you? You really don't know about the money. Kiko, he drew one up recently and left you a lot."

"I'm sick of your shit. Get out of here."

I shrugged and stood. "If they don't prove it was you—"

"It wasn't, asshole."

"But you don't need the money anyway," I said. "You run that restaurant in New Orleans."

His eyes narrowed.

I started for the door, opened it, and turned back to him. "Had a great meal with a wonderful woman tonight, Luz Soccorro."

We stood staring at each other.

"She'd be disappointed you didn't offer me a beer, Kiko."

I turned and walked out.

# Chapter Twenty-Six

——

STARTING SATURDAY at two under par and tied for 18th place was not what I'd envisioned after an opening round 69. I wanted to rebound from Friday's 73. I had shot worse scores in my career, but it was the way I'd made 73 that bothered me—blowing strokes on the final holes. That said something I didn't like about my concentration, which I so prided myself on. There were better ball strikers and better putters, but no one, I'd always told myself, was mentally tougher. And Friday I had not lived up to my own expectations.

On the first tee, I wore a light jacket. The air was peppered with the lilac aroma of desert shrubs and the gallery was large. People always come to see the weekend action. The field had been cut and even 18th place and ties had a few fans; there were maybe a hundred people watching my twosome. I was playing with Padre Tarbuck, who was also at minus two. Regardless of the day's events, at least the company would be good. Padre was known as one of the best guys with which to be paired: relaxed, cordial, and talkative.

The sky was blue; I knew I would not need the jacket long. There was only a slight breeze. It was perfect scoring weather. I began with two lackluster pars. Par isn't usually a bad score, but after back-to-back 300-yard drives, I had hit poor approach shots consecutively that left birdie putts of 20 feet and a 35 feet, respectively. I had made neither. Padre, however, was heating up. As long as I'd known him, he'd been a streaky putter. When he was hot, watch out. He drilled an eight-footer on the first hole, then sunk a birdie putt from 15 feet on two.

The third hole was a 165-yard par three, which forced you to carry a short- to mid-iron over desert to an elevated, pear-shaped, three-tiered green. On this day, the pin was on the top plateau, only four paces from the left collar and a greenside bunker. We stood on the tee and watched the group in front of us putt out.

I said: "You've got the flat stick going today."

Padre raised a finger to his thin lips. "The putter might hear you and wake up."

He was first to hit and selected what appeared to be a five-wood. We were hitting into the wind; so I figured the 165 yards would play like 200. Padre's ball rose, then seemed to hit a transparent wall in front of the green and dropped down, short of the putting surface. I was longer than Padre and could hit a four-iron.

I knew the shot was good the moment it left the clubface. The contact had been absolutely pure; I felt nothing, as if making a practice swing.

"Sounded like a gunshot," Perkins said.

When the ball landed, the gallery went wild.

"Three feet," Padre said.

After chipping on, he ran his eight-foot par putt well by but made the come-backer for a bogey; he was cooling off.

I had three feet, straight uphill. You couldn't ask for anything easier—which made it challenging. The golf gods were making an effort to get me going—a confidence booster. I crouched behind the ball, and studied the line. Straight in. Except when I stood over the ball, I had to back away.

My mind had run to Hutch Gainer.

I envisioned him sitting in his jail cell, thin and pale—and innocent. I thought of his crimes—he had committed some against the Tour, against me even—but he hadn't murdered anyone. Yet, as Lisa said, the evidence still pointed to him. And Chee still had him locked up.

"What's wrong?" Perkins said. "You look confused."

"My mind's going a mile a minute." I took the towel off the bag and wiped my face.

Dyslexics are typically driven and single-minded. I was no different: once I set my mind to something, I don't stop until I finish. In grade school my teachers used to get angry when I'd draw pictures of golf holes instead of taking notes. I nearly failed the college class for which I first read *Hamlet* because I stopped following the syllabus after that—I read the *Complete Works of Shakespeare* cover to cover instead. Typically, all of this carries over to golf. But golf is usually my life's focus. Now, as had happened during my previous round, several things fought for my total attention.

I slid a dime under my ball to mark it, then replaced it, aligning the Titleist brand name as if it were a stripe. I took a deep breath, made no practice strokes, and hit the putt. If I had brought the club back and through straight, the Titleist insignia would have rolled in a tight spiral, becoming a blurred stripe.

My stroke produced the wobble of a lop-sided egg. I made par and stayed at two-under par.

\* \* \*

The next 15 holes were painful. I tried to think about golf, told myself I owed it to me, the fans, and the Tour to give my best effort. The fact was that my mind was on Hutch, Kiko, and Jenna, Ron Giacomin and Rosselli, and of course the man hired to kill me, Joey Chrissani. So my best effort was piss poor.

What made it so frustrating was that this was new to me. The only other time I had difficulty concentrating during a competitive round had been when I'd learned my father had been stricken with a heart attack. That had been years ago. I had let Kiko and Giacomin disrupt my previous round; now I was letting my own mind get to me. I felt like things were coming to a head, like something had to give: neither Lisa nor I, nor Perkins, nor Chee could go on like this.

I had begun swinging a golf club at age three. Thirty-two years later I thought I knew how every muscle in my body reacted to the various pressures of golf. I hadn't won, but real pressure isn't always about winning; it's about sinking a six-foot putt to make a cut, or nailing a 10-footer to place 20th in a tourney and, thus, keep my playing privileges.

On the 18th green, I had a 10-foot putt to shoot 79. I had never hit 80 in my decade on Tour. That was something of which I was proud. Through wind, rain, even a sleet storm in Texas, I'd maintained some level of consistency. And I would not hit 80 on this day. Regardless of Hutch, gambling, or Chrissani.

"Tough day," Perkins said.

"Golf's a mental game," I said. "You can't control your own mind, you can't play."

"Don't be so tough on yourself. Padre isn't doing much better."

He was even par; his card held four birdies and four bogeys.

I took my putter from Perkins and walked to various points on the green, surveying my putt. My hands were pools of perspiration; my hat was saturated; my shirt—navy blue—was now black; and my khaki pants were damp. It was low-70s but I felt like we were in Georgia in July. This 10-footer was downhill and off a plateau: it would be quick and dart hard to the left.

The gallery surrounded the green. Some of the people I vaguely recognized as having followed Padre and me. Others sat in folding chairs and had camped there for the day. Then I saw them—Kiko and Chrissani. Kiko was on one end of the front row of spectators, Joey on the other.

Logic said Chrissani wasn't going to make a hit in front of a gallery. So they were there only to intimidate—again. Which added insult to injury.

I walked to the right edge of the green, turned my back to them, and crouched behind the ball. I marked it, then realigned my ball, and stood. The bastards wouldn't win. I took a practice stroke. All my senses were heightened. I heard my own breath rasp; my chest was tight; my head ached.

I looked down the line. The putt would be fast; the safe play was to hit the ball off the toe of the putter to deaden the blow in an attempt to stop it any place close, and take my two-putt 80.

But 80 was unacceptable. I had nearly lost Lisa because of all this. Gambling had reached the game men played with honor and integrity. And now two thugs watched me with the intent of intimidating.

As I brought the putter back, someone yelled *You The Man!* It was Chrissani.

The ball hit the back of the cup hard, leaped into the air, and fell into the hole with a clatter like change into a tin can.

A marshal was already approaching him. I pointed at Joey. "That was for you."

The gallery cheered wildly.

\* \* \*

Later, my hotel suite was silent. Perkins sat on the loveseat, slouched; Chee leaned against the wall, contemplating. On the edge of a chair, in my gym shorts, I sipped a beer and considered a shower. Neither the air conditioner nor TV was on, nor did anyone speak for several minutes.

Then Chee said to me: "Your hand is shaking," and motioned

toward my Heineken bottle.

I looked down at the rich green bottle. It trembled.

"I could put my fist through a fucking wall right now," I said.

"Jack, there's nothing I can do," Chee said. "The evidence still points to Hutch."

"Not that. Golf. I was in fifth place 48 hours ago," I said. "I'm almost dead goddamned last now."

"Your livelihood." Chee nodded. "I understand."

"No you don't. People think it's a job. But it's not. If I could leave it at the course I probably wouldn't be out there."

Neither Chee nor Perkins said anything.

I went on: "And I may or may not still be engaged."

Chee looked uncomfortable.

Perkins said: "And Hutch Gainer didn't do it and but you've still got him sitting in jail."

\* \* \*

The shower did less than the beer to help me relax. Scores of 69, 73, and 79 had me five shots over par on a course the field was scorching. The hot water sluiced over me as I worked on my second beer. Why would Kiko be working with Chrissani? Joey was Rosselli's man, and Kiko was Giacomin's, or had been the day before when he had been freelancing. And supposedly Rosselli had hired Chrissani to kill me. If that was the case, Frank must have sent them both to the golf course. He had never called to set up our chat. Was he through talking?

I turned off the water, dressed, and returned to the living room, wearing jeans and a blue T-shirt that said FOOTJOY across the back. The drapes of the sliding glass door were open, allowing an evening breeze. The sun was setting.

"I ordered two steaks," Perkins said. "Yours is well done."

"Thanks."

Chee was still there, seated on the desk chair now. "Kiko must be with Rosselli now."

"Yeah," I said.

The phone rang.

I answered: "Jack Austin."

"Go to the pay phone in the lobby. Go there alone and don't try a fucking thing. Lisa's life depends on it." There was a pause, then Lisa: "J—Jack." Another pause, then Chrissani's voice again: "If you want to see her again, you'll do exactly what I tell you."

I tried to hold my voice steady: "Be right there." I hung up.

"Who was that?" Perkins said.

Lisa had been frightened. And I had seen firsthand what Joey Chrissani was capable of. "Dempsey," I said, "wants me to run to his room for a second. Sign some contract."

"I'll go with you," Perkins said.

"No. He's just down the hall. Somebody's got to wait for the food."

"Chee can."

"No, no. I'll be right back."

"Jack—"

"If they were going to try something they'd have done it on the course."

"No, they—"

"Dempsey isn't setting me up," I said and walked out of the room. And sprinted to the stairwell.

* * *

"Here's how this'll work." Chrissani's voice was harsh and the words came rapidly. "You hang up, go back and wait for the cop to leave, get rid of the goddamned football player. Then meet us—alone—in the lobby at midnight. If you do that, Lisa walks. If you don't—she'll feel pain very few people experience."

When I had heard Lisa's sobs in the background, he had won.

* * *

On the elevator returning to my room, I stood staring at the floor. How had they known Chee was in my room? Why hadn't Rosselli made the threat? Frank had said he didn't trust Chrissani. Yet Joey seemed to be running this. Maybe Rosselli knew pain was Chrissani's specialty and had simply turned the entire operation over to him. But something didn't seem right about that theory. Could Chrissani have moved to Frank's number-two spot? He had to be better than Gianni.

They had Lisa.

But I knew about Rosselli: betting; killing the guy in front of his family; and killing the homeless man.

They were after me. But they had Lisa now. She had been dragged into this from the start without knowing the severity of it all. She had persevered and chased down much of her story, not knowing this would ever happen. I hadn't dictated Hutch's appearance in my life. But the night he'd first come to my room I could've thrown him out. Was my involvement selfish? I, like many dyslexics, had always seen the world in black and white terms. I was to marry Lisa. Golf was my livelihood. Before Lisa, it had been my life since I could walk nine holes. Was it still my life? Or was Lisa?

A man's life and the game's integrity had been at stake. Had it been unrealistic to have thought I could save both? Yes.

I needed Lisa Trembley in my life. Again selfish. But true. She made me whole. I loved her, like no one or nothing else. And that included golf.

# Chapter Twenty-Seven

—

I HAD NEVER CONSIDERED TELLING Perkins or Chee about the call. Someone had followed or was watching me. I would do what I'd been told to do. And in order to do what he had demanded, I had to say I was going to bed early. After the way I had played, that was understandable. So Chee left. I asked Perkins to get his own room for the night. I told him that I was tired and upset and I needed to be alone. I had his beeper number. He agreed and said he was going to watch Kiko, maybe even talk to him. I warned him to be careful.

When they were gone, I sat thinking. My thoughts were awful. Lisa was with Chrissani and Rosselli, two sociopaths. Golf wasn't an issue anymore: I was no longer in contention, now playing merely for pride, but that didn't matter. Neither did Hutch Gainer. They had Lisa.

A spare 60-degree wedge leaned against the wall with some balls. With the ball positioned near my back foot, I brought the club up and down on a steep angle, sliding the clubface sharply under it, popping it into the air and onto the bed—your standard bunker shot. I didn't clear my mind, but relaxed some of the muscles in my shoulders.

The digital clock read 3:29.

I did a double take: 9:32. I had reversed the numbers. Still two and a half more hours.

Rosselli was obviously luring me into something. I chipped a second ball. When he wanted to talk, he did. Like at Lisa's home.

—

He wanted me to come alone. I was smart enough to assume he didn't plan on allowing either Lisa or me to walk away; Joey Chrissani was here for a reason. Disappearance was his specialty and—given our public careers—we required that.

The back of my neck was wet with perspiration, so I went out to the balcony and sat beneath a black sky. I remembered the first time I'd seen Lisa. She had interviewed me after a round and had been stunningly beautiful, as always, and confident as hell. We had argued about my putting woes. Yet, after I'd stormed off, I hadn't been able to get her out of my mind. I had never been able to.

At 35, I was single and in a profession which required complete and total focus. The stroke-inflation scandal had taught me that Lisa's job was very similar to mine: I struggled semiannually to keep my playing privileges; she fought to remain in a high-ranking man's world. Given the demands placed on us by our chosen careers, marriage would be a big step. But, as Padre had said, we were good together.

And I loved Lisa. With every ounce of my soul, I loved her. She made me laugh and, at times, made me swear. I needed her.

But Frank had hired Chrissani. And now they had her.

* * *

At 10 minutes to 12, wearing khaki pants and the baggy wind-breaker, I opened the door a crack. The small .22 was flat and it had tucked into my athletic sock nicely, to the inside of my right ankle. There was no one in direct view, so I stepped out and was not ambushed.

The elevator was to my right. I went left—the same thing that had occurred driving to Santa Fe with Lisa for dinner. In my mind's eye, I could see the elevator and where I was, but not how to get from point A to B. I cursed, glanced at the numbers on the doors to position myself, and headed in the right direction.

When I turned the corner near the elevator, I froze.

Grant Ashley stood, in shorts, T-shirt, and bare feet, looking at me.

"What are you doing here?" I said.

Behind him were three putters resting against the wall—an Arnold Palmer blade, a mallet-headed Zebra, and a long putter. On the royal blue carpet, were some golf balls and a water glass.

"What kind of question is that?" He took the long putter, positioned it beneath his chin, and rocked it back and forth.

I said: "Just surprised to see you."

"You're white as a sheet. You ought to get to bed." He rolled a ball. In the silent hallway, it sounded like a wind chime as it struck the back of the glass.

\* \* \*

I stopped the elevator between floors, took several deep breaths, and rechecked the load on the .22. Now I was jumpy walking through hotels. This had to end, and soon. I took inventory: the khakis were baggy and concealed the handgun effectively. I knew my hair was disheveled, my eyes pink with tiny veins, and I needed a shave; my hands were clammy and seemed to move as if thinking for themselves. And a bead of sweat ran down the left side of my face. Grant had been right: I ought to be in bed.

The elevator doors opened.

Chrissani stood smiling. He wore a brown leather jacket, jeans, and cowboy boots with silver tips. His brown hair was gelled. He had on cologne.

"This a date?" I said.

"With destiny. Been here all evening—saw the cop and the football player leave. That's good. Come this way, golf boy."

He was a killer. I should not follow.

Lisa's smile; her laugh; her touch. I went.

\* \* \*

The black Suburban was at the far end of the parking lot, running. For an instant, the dome light went on inside—Lisa sat looking at me through the window—then the inside of the vehicle went black.

"Chrissani," I said.

We stopped.

I raised a finger and pointed. "If you—"

"Save it," he said. "I've heard it before. If I hurt her, you'll kill me."

I have no explanation for what followed. My actions were those of a sleepwalker obeying voices we stifle until they become screams. Something tightened in my neck, like a balloon, hot and tense, and swelled until I saw nothing, except my right fist flash and explode against his left cheek. He went down. Then sat up quickly. Blood trickled from his lip.

Chrissani smiled from the ground. "Two ways to do this, Motherfucker. Quick or slow. You just chose the second option."

Gianni, wearing a gray suit and polished black winged tips that shone beneath the parking lot lights, was out of the truck, running toward us, gun in hand, as Chrissani climbed to his feet.

"Put that away," Joey said. "Jesus Christ." He looked around. "Tommy, what are you doing? Put that away and pat him down."

"Tommy," a voice called from behind.

"Shit," Joey said.

"Tommy, where's Frank?" Jenna came out of the hotel behind us.

"Take him to the truck," Gianni said. "I'll get rid of her."

"Let's go," Chrissani said.

Maybe hitting Chrissani hadn't been a bad idea. Things were not going smoothly; I wanted to stall the operation further.

Jenna got closer and repeated her question.

"Frank—had to—leave town—this afternoon," Gianni said.

"I saw him in the lobby at 5:00."

"Yeah, right after that."

"What's going on?" Jenna said. "Where's Kiko?"

The parking lot was empty of people and scattered with vehicles. We were not directly under a lamp, but the lights around us cast long shadows, and I took it all in like a spectator at a street production.

"Jenna," Gianni said, "get out of here."

"Tell me."

"Listen," Joey said, "I'm losing my fucking patience with this whole thing."

"Not a smooth hit, when you get dropped by the hittee," I said.

"You'll get yours." He turned to Jenna. "Frank's gone and that's it."

"When's he coming back?" she said.

Joey shook his head and pushed me forward, except he couldn't; I stood my ground.

Jenna's gaze fell on Gianni who simply smiled.

"You killed him. Just like you killed Johnny."

"Jenna," I said, "get out of here. Leave town."

"Enough." Gianni raised the gun and waved it around. "Enough. We're following my plan."

"Put that away," Joey said. "Are you coked up?"

"You're a prick, Tommy," Jenna said.

"And you're a cheap whore." He pushed her and she stumbled and fell.

Joey shoved his coat pocket against my back. I felt the pointed end of a barrel.

Gianni turned and we headed to the truck, leaving Jenna on the ground. Lisa must have watched the whole scene from the second seat and it must've played out like an Absurdist drama. Kiko sat behind her in the third seat. Joey's boots made a tapping sound and Gianni's suit pants swooshed back and forth as we walked.

The dome light came on again. My eyes met Lisa's. She wore jeans and a light jacket over a pink top. Her mascara had run and smudged on her cheeks; her hair was disheveled. As she raised a hand to rub her eye, it trembled. But she gave a tiny nod and the look in her eyes told me she was stronger than even I had known.

"Get in." Joey held the door.

I sat very close to her; Joey got behind the wheel; and Gianni climbed in the passenger seat. I heard only the sound of breathing when the doors shut.

I leaned over and kissed her forehead.

"Sweet," Gianni said.

The truck began moving.

"I don't like it," Joey said. "You shouldn't be jacked up when we're doing this. That's how people accidentally get shot."

"We're back on time," Gianni said. "My schedule's fine."

"Something has to be done about Jenna."

"Where's Frank?" I said.

Gianni said over his shoulder: "We're taking you to meet him." I could see the side of his face. He could barely contain his smirk.

"Witty."

He turned to look at me. "*I* thought so."

"You go through his closet?"

"You could say that."

"But you don't look comfortable in his suit."

He didn't respond.

"It's a metaphor, Gianni. You can't run Frank's business. You're not good enough. You'd struggle pushing pills on a street corner."

He spun around again. Now his face was flushed and his gun was drawn.

Lisa gasped.

"Tommy, we're in a moving fucking vehicle," Joey said. "Don't do anything stupid. Austin, shut the hell up."

"I've been watching Frank make mistakes for years," Gianni said. "I can do better."

My knowledge of Albuquerque's streets was limited. I only

knew the surrounding highways—40 and 25. The inside of the truck was dark and we seemed to be hitting a lot of traffic lights.

"They killed Rosselli," Lisa whispered.

"You see it?"

"No, but—"

"Shut up," Gianni said. He was facing front again.

"Why? Is it a secret?" I said. "You afraid we'll—"

Gianni wheeled around and pointed his gun again. "You—shut—up—right—now." His hand quivered and veins emerged on his forehead. Joey was right: Gianni was cranked up.

"Jesus, Tommy," Kiko said. "Put that fucking thing away. I'm back here."

"Yeah, relax, Tommy," Joey said. "We'll stop, get you some beer. Help you relax. Give me the gun."

Smirking again, Gianni handed him the pistol. He ran his hand through his hair.

We hit a light and stopped again. Inside the truck, the air seemed heavy with the lemon-and-grease-like odor of perspiration.

"So," I said, "Hutch Gainer will take the fall for Joey shooting Pickorino."

"No." Kiko said it quickly from behind.

"No he won't take the fall, or no he didn't kill Pickorino?"

"Everyone stop talking," Joey said.

"Gianni," I said, "shouldn't you be saying that?"

"You're going to die tonight, Austin," Gianni said. "Is that saying enough?"

Lisa took my hand and shook her head, signaling me to be quiet. But they weren't going to shoot anyone in the truck. We were going someplace for that purpose. The doors were locked. I glanced over my shoulder. Through the dark, I saw Kiko's hands in his lap. His rings shone, but I didn't see a gun.

# Chapter Twenty-Eight

———

We stopped at a light again.

I said: "So, Gianni, you recruit Kiko to kill John Pickorino and frame Hutch Gainer."

No one answered.

"But now Joey, the specialist is, here. Kiko going to be your accountant?"

"Shut up," Gianni said.

"Hey, Kiko," I said, "not a lot of job security in that response. Maybe we drive out to the desert with five people and, instead of three, only two come back."

"I'm getting tired of your mouth," Joey said.

"Why Pickorino?" I said. "Frank was making money from him. You had to see some of that money."

The truck went silent.

Then Gianni chuckled.

I saw the back of his head as he shook it. "Jesus Christ, you don't know a fucking thing."

Lisa raised her brows, listening intently; she was still on the story.

"Everyone stop talking," Joey said.

"I've got the whole thing figured out," I said.

Gianni glanced at Joey, who shrugged as if it didn't matter.

I wasn't sure exactly what happened, but figured if I gave some explanation, Gianni might be proud enough of his master plan to elaborate. "Pickorino was blackmailing Hutch Gainer and costing Frank money. You hated Frank anyway, Gianni, because he treated you like a little brother instead of his right-hand man. Although cokeheads don't make good right-hand men."

"I got sick of him. He had to be—eliminated." He turned to face me and smiled, proud of finding the perfect word. "I'm getting sick of you, too. And your story's already wrong."

"Tommy, he doesn't need information," Joey said.

"What's the difference?" I said.

"I," Gianni said, "blackmailed Gainer."

Silence again.

He smiled. "I've seen Frank play horses—he always knew who had run well the week before."

"So after a good round," I said, "you'd send a note, hoping Frank would bet on the next. You used his research against him."

No one spoke.

I said: "You figured you'd gotten even—costing Frank money—and you thought if you could outsmart the boss, hell, you could run the entire show. So you got Kiko to take out Pickorino." I turned to Kiko. "But you had a decent thing with Pickorino. What was the offer?"

Kiko had not moved. Sitting quietly, he glanced at Gianni. I did the same. He was smiling like a kid, proud of his scheme. Then he motioned for Kiko to answer.

"The number-two position."

"You had that with Pickorino."

"And now I've got it with Pickorino's operation and Rosselli's," Kiko said.

The back of Joey's head was still. Outside, we were beyond street lamps and traffic. The area was becoming rural.

"Joey did Rosselli in exchange for what?" I said.

"That's enough talk," Joey said.

He glanced in the rearview mirror. Our eyes met. We both knew Gianni needed only one number-two man. We also knew Joey wouldn't settle for number-two status long.

The truck turned onto a dirt road.

"Three more miles," Gianni said.

*　*　*

We drove in the dark for a long time. Three miles across a moonlit dirt road takes time. Rocks, sticks, and gravel crunched. The headlights illuminated rising dust and desert landscape. In the silence of the truck, I held Lisa's hand. Now we both knew exactly what had happened—which made the gravity of our situation palpable.

I thought. My mind immediately went to Lisa, as if fleeing the present uncertainty. But that was useless. I had a pistol. It was small and I was inexperienced. But these men were planning to kill us.

I freed my hand from Lisa's.

Gianni had lost his gun to Joey, with whom I wanted no part in a gunfight. But Joey was driving; if I was ever going to take him, now was the time. I glanced behind me. In the rear, Kiko sat looking out the window, his hands remained in his lap, still and empty.

I moved away from Lisa, leaned forward only slightly, and grabbed the .22, freeing the safety as I went.

I sat with my right hand—and gun—beneath my leg.

Lisa stared straight ahead.

"There's an orange mark on the telephone pole," Gianni said. "Kiko, where the hell is it?"

"Keep going," Kiko said.

I slid all the way to my right, leaned back against the door so I could see all three, and raised the gun, pointing it at Joey Chrissani's temple. "Stop the truck slowly and put on the dome light."

"What're you talking about?" Gianni said over his shoulder. Then he looked. "Where'd you—"

The truck stopped.

Behind me, Kiko said: "Jesus Christ." I glanced over my shoulder to see him reach inside his coat.

"No." I wheeled and pointed the gun.

He froze. In an instant, I wheeled back to the other two, then back at Kiko again, inadvertently pointing the gun at Lisa. "Put your hands on your head."

Kiko did.

I pushed back against the door to cover all three. "No one even breathe," I said. "Lisa, get out."

She opened her door and climbed down, facing the truck as she backed away maybe ten yards.

The ceiling light had not come on.

"This is how things'll work," I said. My voice rasped and my breath was short. Joey had yet to look at me. He sat staring strait ahead like a defiant school kid, as if this was his game and he wasn't going to lose.

"Joey," I said, "put your hands on your head."

His hands were on the wheel. He left them there. My thought

had been to take the gun off his lap first. But Kiko had not allowed that to happen—he had gone for his own gun, forcing me to deal with that. If I went for Joey's gun now, Kiko would make a move. If he didn't, Gianni was coked up and crazy enough to try something. I didn't want that, especially with Lisa still nearby. Besides, my gun was on Joey.

The air was heavy, thick with tension as I thought. I didn't want to get in the third seat—that was too far away from Joey and Gianni in the front to allow me constant view of their hands. Yet I didn't want to have to look over my shoulder to keep an eye on Kiko, who—although his hands were on his head—still had a gun inside of his coat. So I would move Kiko next to me in the second row, then take his gun.

We sat like that for several long moments: Kiko, his hands on his head; Joey, the gun on his lap, but his hands on the wheel; and me, gun pointed at Joey, frequent glances at Kiko, mind racing.

"Kiko," I said, "you move beside me."

In hindsight, moving Kiko to the middle seat wasn't a plan that Perkins would have invented. The commotion of his movement would have left Gianni and Joey with too many options.

"Kiko," Gianni said, "you stay there."

Joey moved his hands down the sides of the steering wheel.

"Put—them—in—the—air," I said.

He froze and moved his hands slowly upward.

"Kiko," I said, "move up."

"Kiko, don't do it."

"Gianni," I said, "shut up."

Joey moved his right hand down, then up.

I saw a flash of metal and my finger squeezed, the reaction unconscious.

The noise of the blast drowned out the sound of Lisa's shriek. Gianni began to curse and the horn went off as Joe's body slumped forward. The truck began to roll.

I shoved my gun into Gianni's ear. My hand shook violently.

"Put it in Park."

"Fuck you."

I grabbed a handful of hair and jerked the gun hard into his ear. Blood trickled out. Beads of sweat ran into my eyes.

"I can't—stop—my—hand—from—shaking. And my finger's— on—the—trigger." I looked back again. Kiko hadn't moved. His face held the look of a guy who had crapped out and was waiting for the next hand.

Gianni, his left arm on the console, leaned over and ground the gearshift on the steering column into Park. The truck halted.

In the light, the back of Joey's head was matted and dark with blood. Otherwise, the small caliber handgun had done little damage—the bullet must have rattled around inside his skull because it had not exited through the windshield.

"Kiko," Gianni said, "don't you leave that fucking seat."

"Kiko," I said, "I'm shooting you in five seconds if you're not beside me."

"Kiko—"

Kiko hunched too far forward, as if bending to stand, but overdone. His hand was on its way out of his jacket.

I lunged toward him and shoved my pistol beneath his chin. He froze. I reached into Kiko's jacket and pulled out his gun. "Lisa, watch Gianni."

She moved close to the truck. I didn't like that, but there were two of them—one, a killer with perhaps another gun I needed to take; the other, crazy enough to try anything. She opened the door slowly and looked past the corpse to Gianni, her eyes fixated on him.

I felt farther inside Kiko's jacket. Nothing.

The scent of gunpowder was strong and it overtook the other odors that must have been present.

To check Kiko's pants, I had to lean forward, which put my own head below his—a vulnerable position. As I leaned down, I pushed my gun up harder into the soft tissue beneath his chin, straightening his spine.

There was a bulge above his right ankle. I pulled up his pant leg. It was an ankle holster and I took that gun, too, and sat back against my door.

The inside of the truck was silent, except for tense breathing. Joe's corpse threw a kink in my plans—someone would have to get out and pull it from the truck.

I couldn't ask Lisa to do that.

"Gianni," I said, "open your door slowly and stand outside."

"Why?"

"You're going to take Joey out and clean the seat."

"Fuck you."

I raised the .22 to Gianni's head. The look of defeat and curiosity had returned to Kiko's face.

The door opened and Gianni stepped out. I quickly followed out the rear door and tossed Kiko's guns into darkness.

We moved around the front of the truck, slowly.

Gianni stopped suddenly.

As he turned toward me, his arm rising, a single thought flashed through my mind: the gun on Joey's lap.

I never gave him a chance. From pointblank, the bullet took him squarely in the chest and knocked him back. Lisa's scream echoed and combined with the gunshot, like a thunderclap over my head. Gianni lay at my feet, face up. One hand lay open in the dirt, the gun visible. I kicked it away.

\* \* \*

Lisa was in my arms. We stood in the headlight.

"Kiko," I said, "I got no problem leaving three stiffs here."

He sat motionless beneath the dome light. "Yeah," he said. "Never took you for the type that could do it."

"Never been forced before," I said. I moved to the driver's side, very carefully reached into Joey's jacket pocket and removed the gun I had felt against my back earlier that evening in the parking lot. "Drag him out."

Kiko rose slowly and moved out from behind the third seat. I watched as the body flopped unto the desert floor. The corpse's head left a streak of blood on the door window.

"You mind?" He lifted Joe's wallet.

I watched as Kiko took the bills and credit cards. It was a desperate measure and one that spoke volumes about Kiko and his life, where he had come from and where he was headed.

"Get the blood off the door," I said. The seat did not need cleaning.

"With what?"

"Your sleeve."

"Fuck." He did it.

Overhead, the clouds had cleared and the moon was full. On the ride out, no one spoke. Kiko sat in the third seat. I was in the front seat beside Lisa as she drove, my gun and eyes never leaving him.

At the end of the dirt road, I said: "Lisa, stop at the first convenience store. We'll call Chee."

"Yes."

Kiko sighed.

# Chapter Twenty-Nine

—

FOR LISA AND ME, the rest of the night consisted of driving with Perkins and Chee to the station, answering questions, and giving statements. Chee said he wanted to make certain Kiko didn't get off and asked us to give our word that we'd both testify. We did. It was quarter to six when we finally walked out of police headquarters into the presunrise dawn. It felt like bursting through a small opening into the vastness of promise.

The ordeal was over.

The Tour Commissioner and Hutch Gainer's counsel were to meet later that morning.

Lisa and I held hands; Perkins stood beside us.

Jenna Andrews passed us running up the stairs into the building. "Where's Kiko?"

"Inside," Perkins said.

She dashed off.

"She needs somebody," I said.

"Sad," Lisa said, "isn't it?"

"Glad it isn't me she needs," Perkins said.

The morning air was fresh and crisp. The streets were empty and gleamed. Lisa's hair was out of sorts, her mascara still smeared, her clothes wrinkled. She looked beautiful.

"Want to sit here," I said, "watch the sun come up, and I'll get us some breakfast burritos when the street vendors come out?"

"Sounds romantic," she said. "But, I've got my story now. I've got to go to work. Chee said he'd have the hotel send a shuttle over."

"The press hasn't gotten wind of this yet," I said. "It's all yours." I took her hand and we moved down the granite steps, closer to the street. At the bottom, she gave me a long kiss. Perkins sensed the moment and moved away.

When we broke, she said: "I really thought I was going to die last night, Jack."

I didn't say anything.

"When they came and got me, Gianni told me he was going to kill us both."

"They didn't hurt you?"

"No. Did you think we were going to die?"

"I don't know. I knew there was nothing to lose."

"You killed two men."

"Yes," I said.

"And?"

"They were bad people. And they were planning to kill you, which translates to: everything that matters for me."

"Sounds more selfish than heroic."

"It's the honest answer."

"I love you," she said. "You saved my life. That's heroic enough for me."

"I love you, too."

The shuttle arrived.

"Coming?" she said.

I shook my head. "I've got to go to work, too. People in last place play before the gallery shows up."

"Don't think of it like that. Most people would've withdrawn."

"It's still last place," I said.

"I love you." She got into the van.

As she did, the sun seemed to time its appearance perfectly, peaking over the Sandia Mountains and catching her hair with a quick splash, turning it auburn. Her tiny features seemed very delicate, and belied the toughness that had helped her make it through the previous night. I watched the van go and thought of the scenario: two people, engaged to be married, having survived a planned execution, and both rushing off to work like a typical day.

Something was wrong with that.

\* \* \*

The locker room was nearly empty at 7:30 and, of those few present, no one knew of the previous night, which was fine with me. On this morning, as I entered the locker room, sunlight, pure and golden, seemed to nip at my heels. The fresh scent of home-baked tortillas was present. I had showered, changed into fresh clothes, ate huge amounts, and drank coffee.

It was a new day, the launch of a second season for me. I opened a box of shoes and stepped into them. The new leather was stiff, the laces taut and unworn. I took a crisp white glove out of its package, and two sleeves of unblemished balls. Everything new. Outside, on the practice green, a rep was having players try a new line of putters. One was a dark high-hosseled blade like Gary Player used. I grabbed it.

* * *

At eight A.M., after only a handful of warm-up balls, Perkins and I stood on the first tee with a big kid named Jarvis, a Monday Qualifier. He was taller than me, but not as thick, with a patchy beard. We shook hands.

"It's last place," he said. "But still a couple grand. That's good enough."

I could see why he was playing Monday qualifiers, but I ignored it and hit my drive.

Perkins said: "You ought to stay up all night more often."

The shot left me 135 yards to the green, 142 to the flagstick—a hard nine-iron. Only three kids, no older than 10, followed us. Two were obviously twins—both blonde with glasses, and dressed in identical tiny golf shirts, and navy blue shorts—and the third was chubby black kid with a round face. They laughed, swung imaginary golf clubs, and seemed in constant motion. The sun was bright and cast long shadows across the sprawling fairway. My ball was visible in the center the entire walk: a very nice sight. The air carried the sweet aroma of the desert and my shoes made swishing noises on the dewy grass.

Perkins had called the airline from the locker room. His flight left at 3:00. We paused to watch Jarvis hit. He missed the green left.

I turned to Perkins: "Hey," I said, "thank you. You didn't have to take this case."

He waved it off.

"No," I said, "I mean it. Thank you."

"You going to cry on me?"

I checked the kids—watching Jarvis—so I gave Perkins the finger.

"That's better," he said. "That's the level I like to keep things on."

"You get paid by Hutch?"

"Not yet."

"You don't sound worried."

"I've got 25 grand sitting in a college fund for Jackie. That's pretty good."

"Almost forgot about that."

When we reached my ball, I went back to work and spent a lot of time preparing to hit my nine-iron. The ball hit the green, bounced twice, then sat six feet from the pin.

The three young kids walking beside us cheered wildly.

It made me smile. "How are you doing, guys? Let's have some fun out here. How about the wave?" I started it. They went nuts: cheering and doing the wave.

Perkins and I laughed.

I took the bag from Perkins and unzipped a pocket, grabbed some balls and a glove and went to them like Santa. The gifts led to more laughter, leaping, and hollering. I asked them to be quiet when the players hit—they promised to do so—and I left them before I got hurt.

On the green, I stood over the six-footer for birdie, exhaled slowly, and stroked the putt. No reading greens, no analyzing breaks, just a solid, firm stroke with the new putter. The ball went in, center cut.

I shot 33 on the front.

\* \* \*

Perkins and I were on the 18th green. I had carded three additional birdies on the back and was five under par on the day. I was no longer in last place.

"This 12-footer would put me at minus six today," I said. "Be nice to shoot the low round of the day."

"Sixty-seven?"

"That won't hold up," I said. "Weather's ideal. I need to make this for a 66."

"This break?" he said.

"Two balls, left to right."

The kids had stayed with us all morning. One gave me thumbs up. I returned the gesture, and looked the putt over from behind the hole, then addressed the ball. I hit the putt well and it took the break, hit the left edge, and spun out.

I tapped in for a 67.

\* \* \*

When we got back to the locker room it was alive. The contenders were in different stages of preround preparation: some stretched; some did sit-ups on the carpet; some ate breakfast and read the paper. On a big-screen TV, Lisa's face appeared. She was standing on the steps of the police station.

I knew what was coming and moved closer. Several players read BREAKING NEWS on the screen and approached the TV.

Lisa wore a gray suit and did not look like someone who had spent the previous night thinking about death.

"This is Lisa Trembley for CBS Sports. Last week, CBS Sports was the first to bring you the story of Hutch Gainer's score inflation. Last night, that story exploded when this reporter and Tour player Jack Austin were abducted and taken to the desert to be killed. Austin was targeted for attempting to help Gainer; I was kidnapped and used to lure Austin to the attempted killers. In a heroic effort, Austin shot and killed two men, and subdued the third. In the ensuing dialogue, the following story came out..."

Lisa gave the details—how Hutch had set up Pickorino, how he had been blackmailed, how my beating had been a warning. Then she tied Frank and Gianni in, and finished with last night. I watched and listened in awe, as she eloquently summarized nearly two months in a three-minute soliloquy.

Several players turned and stared at me as she spoke.

Padre appeared at my side. "Sixty-seven on top of that. You're my hero, too."

"Even Hamlet had to sleep," I said and turned and headed back to my hotel.

# Chapter Thirty

——

I WAS THE LAST PASSENGER to board the plane, and shoved my carry-on into an overhead compartment.

Lisa, reading the *New York Times*, looked up and smirked upon seeing me. "Oversleep, did we?"

She had on a lavender pantsuit, her black hair pulled up and pinned atop her head; she wore gold hoop earrings the size of silver dollars. She folded the paper and placed it on her lap. Her legs were crossed before her, as she used the additional room that first-class provided.

"Yeah. Never heard the alarm." With my *Complete Works of William Shakespeare*, I took my place—the window seat beside her—and glanced outside. Daybreak was lustrous, as a brilliant sun shone onto the runway. The air inside the plane was stagnant; not yet circulating, and the interior was stuffy. Two guys dressed in dark jumpsuits and thick earmuffs carelessly threw suitcases onto an automatic ramp, which carried them into the belly of the 747.

"There's something I need to discuss," I said.

"Still working on Shakespeare?"

"Yeah. This book will take me through the Senior Tour."

"They suspended Hutch Gainer," she said. "Two years and a million-dollar fine."

"I heard."

"Why are you shaking your head?"

"They're letting him play again later," I said. "He got off easy."

The air in the plane began to circulate; I knew the jet would rumble into action shortly. The overhead air vent began to blow on me.

Lisa opened the *Times* again and began highlighting the text of a golf article.

"Still working?" I asked.

"Making sure no one gets a jump on me."

We rumbled into motion, and headed down the runway. Above Albuquerque, I looked down and saw the golf course.

"Lisa," I said, "I really need—"

"You think a two-year suspension and a million dollars is getting off easy?"

"Yes."

"Everything's always black and white to you, isn't it?"

"It's the way I see things. Always have."

"Dyslexia?" she said.

"I think so."

"Life's choices always seem very clear to you," she said. "As if there're only two sides to everything and you always know exactly where you stand."

"In Hutch's case, it's pretty clear-cut."

"But you helped him."

A flight attendant parked a heavy cart near us. I asked for black coffee; Lisa said hot water with lemon.

"You took on Rosselli to keep the game as pure as you believe it is, didn't you?"

"Don't patronize me," I said.

"I'm not patronizing," she said. "I don't know anyone else who would do that."

She placed her hand on my chin, pulled me near, and kissed me hard on the lips. When we broke, we stayed close to each other for a long moment. My eyes ran to her hand.

The engagement ring was still gone.

"I love you," I said.

"I feel the same way. I saw your eyes—I meant to put the ring on this morning."

"That's what I wanted to talk about," I said. "A lot has happened."

"I never should have said what I did in the bar. I need you near me—always."

"You took the ring off because you weren't sure."

She started to shake her head, then stopped. I sensed we both knew the current plan for our collective future required an amendment. I sat staring at her, thinking I wanted to spend the rest of my life with this woman. Yet, at the same time, I knew we would never have the white house with the porch swing and the picket fence; that lifestyle would suit neither of us.

"Careers are never easy to manage," I said. "We've both chosen ones that demand a lot."

"I don't know if that's why, or if I took it off because I was just angry."

"At me?"

"And the situation—you helping Hutch and not answering my questions."

"That situation reflects who I am."

"And you can't change who you are," she said.

"No one can."

"I don't want you to," she said.

We were quiet for several minutes. The plane had risen above a landscape of clouds that were like mounds of unblemished snow.

"Many golfers have wives," Lisa said. "And many journalists have husbands."

"But not many golfers are married to serious journalists who take great pride and responsibility in being the best at what they do."

"Now you're patronizing me."

"No," I said. "I respect you for it, but that's why I couldn't tell you about Hutch."

"I've been thinking about what would happen if—as unlikely as it sounds—I got assigned off the Tour, or if you ended up playing the Buy.com Tour."

"And?"

"And I thought about requesting a different assignment," she said.

"What?"

"The thought entered my mind. It would make things easier."

"If we were apart?"

"This wouldn't have happened."

"That night during dinner in Maryland," I said. "I saw your goals. I'd never want you to do that."

Her eyes began to pool. She took a deep breath. "It's not the jobs. I know. It's us." She wiped her eyes and sniffled. "I've always put my career before everything and you're just as driven," she said, "and you have your ideals. And, goddamned it, you live by them. And I love you the way you are."

We were flying through the clouds now. They seemed to roll slowly past, huge and inanimate, blotting out the radiant, early morning sun.

"We both went to work yesterday," I said, "like the night before was an everyday occurrence."

She didn't speak.

"Think about that," I said. "It's nearly insane."

She smiled at my word choice and pulled a tissue from her purse beneath her seat.

"Maybe marriage isn't the best option for us," I said, "right now."

Slowly, her head moved up and down. The pools in her eyes spilled over and tears ran down her cheeks.

"Lisa, I'm sorry—"

"No," she said, "you're right. I know it. I just had this image of the white dress, the church." She blew her nose.

I took her hand. "Look at me."

She did.

"Together forever. For me, there is no one else." I reached up and wiped a tear from her cheek. "That's what I'm saying. We'll always be together. I can't imagine being with anyone else. But, right now, it's not a traditional relationship."

"You think it ever will be?"

I leaned close and kissed her. It was a long kiss, one which seemed overdue. When we finished, she smiled, and I thought how I wanted to remember the way she looked at that exact moment forever. I turned and gazed out the window. The clouds were no longer there. Now I saw the sun.

The horizon shone brightly.

# Acknowledgments

———

I WOULD LIKE TO ACKNOWLEDGE several people for helping me in the writing of this novel. At Sleeping Bear Press, publisher Brian Lewis provided a wonderful opportunity. Likewise, I will be forever in debt to editor Danny Freels. Thank you, Danny, for making this a better book and for your support throughout the writing process. Thanks also to Kolleen O'Meara and Carolyn Flintoft at SBP for their behind-the-scenes work. Friend and Tour player J.P. Hayes (it seems annually) takes time from his vacation months to critique my work, a gesture I greatly appreciate. And Allison McClow at PGA Tour Headquarters helped me check my facts. Likewise, PI Sheila Cantor kindly answered my questions about real-life private investigations, and Chris Richards of Caribou Ford in Caribou, Maine for information regarding 4 x 4 transmissions. Dr. Deane Mansfield-Kelly, David Lunde, and Rick DeMarinis, all teachers who offered insight and inspiration. In addition, my parents must be acknowledged in the writing of this book; for, at age nine, I was diagnosed as "learning disabled." Without their encouragement and sacrifices I could have gotten buried like so many others. To them, I owe everything. And, finally, my wife and best friend, Lisa, who puts up with first drafts and my 4 A.M. writing schedule: without your love, support, and friendship this book might not have been written.

———